What Went Missing

and

What Got Found

What Went Missing and What Got Found by Fatima Shaik
Published by Xavier Review Press
1 Drexel Drive
New Orleans, Louisiana 70125

Printed in the United States of America
First Edition

Book cover illustration and author photograph by Sophia Little
Book design: Bill Lavender
Adapted for Ingram editions

Stories in this collection have appeared in
The Southern Review, African-American Fiction
and *Xavier Review*.

Printed in the U.S.A.
10 9 8 7 6 5 4 3 2   15 16 17 18 19 20

Library of Congress Control Number: 2015900076
ISBN 978-1-883275-25-9 (pbk.)

What Went Missing

and

What Got Found

Stories

Fatima Shaik

XAVIEREVIEW
PRESS

To the people who are quick to offer a seat at the table, a plate of food, a favorite song, and good conversation.

Contents

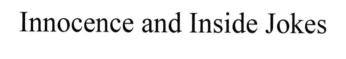

Innocence and Inside Jokes

Charity Begins at Home

The bench inside the front yard fence is a long bench. It's made of wood slats and ornery nails with everything painted over a thick green by hand. It runs across the driveway gate where the cars don't go out anymore. I've heard people call this bench wide.

That always made Mama and Papa stiffen up from where they were sitting, center of the bench, hid in the shade from the sun. Words like wide, broad, heavy or fat are not used in this house. They are much too personal for people in Mama and Papa's condition.

So how can I put it? "We are of sizable portions," I heard Mama say to the lady from mail order over the phone. If people come to the door, I tell them with my hands. I stretch out all the way to the ends of my arms and curve the palms and fingers inward, then I lift my eyes, to say Mama is just upstairs.

We are religious so the people's reactions don't bother us anymore. "The first shall be last and the least shall be first, at the head of the line," Mama has promised me out of the Bible.

In the next life, we plan on being right up in there. This life, we trace from the Garden of Eden.

If I was there, I would not have ate that first bite. I am not partial to apples, never mind snakes. But like Adam and Eve, I am special coming out of creation. I am a special and innocent child for no matter how old I get, Mama said. She told me that over 30 years past when my mind first wouldn't work with my mouth. We could never get me to talk. The things I hear stay inside and don't come back out.

People say I am "Slow" or spin their fingers around one side of their ears and whisper, "Confused."

But God made me in His image and likeness, I heard on the Catholic radio station.

Mama and Papa are sitting out in the yard waiting for news of some poor off kin. Some girl cousin of Mama's got herself pregnant, they say, by one of any number of men.

Of course, nobody tells me that direct. I heard Mama and Papa talking about little cousin and saying, "Poor child, her Mama is liked to died." Papa's repeating, "The sins of the flesh. The sins of the flesh," louder and louder. That's what caught my attention.

I thought it had something to do with the way Mama and Papa were sitting. They were in the same position then as today. They are sitting outside while the sun is still up. And that makes them sweat too much. And sometimes they get stuck together in various parts. And they tell me to go get them some ice that they can rub on their poor, red, welted arms where the heat has made them sweat to bumps and stick their skin together to make them itch.

I run fast as I can to the refrigerator, "the Frigidaire" I like to call it to myself sometimes to show off. I like the way it makes people pause and smile when Mama says that. I wait in the open door with my body next to the empty racks until I cool off. But I don't stand there too long to tempt fate for putting myself first cool instead of least cool and making a sin. Instead, I stand in the Frigidaire and open the little box for the frozen things, and hold that open with my elbow while I try to bust the cubes out of the plastic.

"Who! It's hot out here," I could hear Papa getting restless through the screen door. I bang the ice cube tray on the counter, so they can hear I'm going as fast as I can.

"Don't disrespect your Papa," Mama hollers in response. She likes the neighborhood to know she's a woman of righteous intentions. She always thinks first of her husband.

"Never would find me running the street," she told me stories to prepare for my womanhood. "Not no kind of tramp like they got now days," she repeats. Mama won't let me be like she was, she says. But she don't explain that to me exactly. She would rather tell me what's truth than what's real, she says, like the Bible.

Mama never leaves outside the front gate, and only goes out of the house when Papa comes home from work. She bathes herself at about 4 o'clock. That's when her last tv story goes off and also after she has finally completed her breakfast. She likes to stretch it out with a snack, so she doesn't have to eat lunch.

For dinner, Mama and Papa go outside while I cook. And after I finish the dishes, Mama turns on the radio rosary. It comes from the shrine of St. Jude, the saint of hopeless causes. We pray for the poor, the sick, and the lonely. Some people, the priest says, before he begins his recitation, don't have no one to take care of them.

While we pray, Papa likes to watch the evening news. I can see the pictures jumping across the screen from the place in the next room where I'm sitting. We are separated by two window pane glass doors that Papa latches shut before Mama and I turn on the radio, and he turns on the television. Papa likes to start his beer then too, when he is away from us.

Mama says she can't stop him from drinking while she's saying her prayers to God. Papa says he's a man and he can do anything.

Papa's got a stomach like a watermelon, just like the ones off the vegetable truck. Once the driver stopped in front of our door. I had waved him down when I heard his singing. Papa went outside the gate to the street and brought a big, green, striped melon back.

3

He carried it over one hip in the curve of his side right next to his stomach. As he was walking, I caught his side view, and it looked like to me he could be having a baby or even twins the way the big, round shapes jutted out twice. I patted him in the middle and the melon right at its navel. Then I rocked my arms like a cradle. At first he laughed. Then he looked worried or like he wanted to be angry. Then he got embarrassed. People said I was a twin when I was in my mother's belly.

I know they talk about babies when they are outside, Mama and Papa. That is their private conversation. I heard Mama talking about the unwed mothers and the population explosion. I picture it kind of like a war. All these ladies lie on a field, like the casualties all scattered about. They are all on their backs with their big watermelon stomachs most prominent. Then boom. They burst one by one, like when a ripe melon you drop on the ground explodes, except they would explode up. And out would come these dancing babies, jumping out of their mamas, now like melted balloons on the ground. Babies dancing the Irish jig. Babies dancing the twist. I like babies.

Mama said too many people in the world causes starvation, especially among foreigners. "Look at India," she shows me the snapshots with begging in the newspaper. "And China and Africa," she points her fingers over their bones and their deep shrunk eyes. "These are the least of the least, and they will be first up in heaven." She reminds me how lucky I am. I feel lucky, even though I know that God loves the foreign children better than He loves me.

But I got a lot of love. The priest who gives me communion tells me that he is my brother. And that year that I went to school, a boy named John held my hand in the lunchroom. He was sweaty, and his fingers felt like the joints of chicken where I break up the gristle with the point of the knife. I wash my hands for Salmonella every time, just like my mother told me.

Mama's calling now for my attention. I can hear her, "Loutie. Loutie."

The children in school said it sounded like she was calling a pig. They said I looked like a pig too. I couldn't help but get in that fight. The people told Mama that a girl who can't talk or think straight half the time don't need to know how to read or write no way.

Mama says she's going to die soon. But she's being saying that for more than 30 years. Since I was a child. Mama said I was her hardest birth. I was her only one, except for the boy who never came out. That's why she is so fat right now.

She told me, "Cause of that childbearing. I look a mess like this. Had me a good figure before that. The best figure in town."

Papa says, "Hey yeah," on that one. Makes everybody laugh. They happy, the ones that stand outside the fence and laugh to remember her beautiful pictures. The others that laugh who have not seen the pictures, I think they laugh because she now looks like me and they cannot imagine her bragging about pretty at all. But Mama showed me her photos of when as a girl. She looked like herself in the eyes except then they seemed more important. They were big and dark like to match the black color of hair she keeps in the bathroom drawer. She was a girl, but Papa "was at" her already as she explains it. I could see in the picture. On her waist a man's arm is going off to the side. Papa says it was him. Mama won't speak on that subject. But she likes to take the picture and pin it up on the tree alongside the bench when she sits there if Papa has gone inside.

But most of the time, they sit together. They both talking on little cousin this afternoon.

"She's so stupid," Mama says. "Don't she know they got too many babies in the world," Mama asks Papa like it's not a real question.

"What she going do? Send it back," Papa gives her no kind of answer as usual.

"She never should have open them legs up in the first place," the evil stare Mama gives him I could feel to here.

I have come to agree with her. It's a sin to take pleasure in babies when the world got all those foreign babies who aren't happy at all. We should wait until the foreign babies get happy. Then we could get happy and blessed too because we would have made ourselves the least of all.

I could hear Mama calling and calling, "Loutie. Loutie. Ice Cubes. Today." She's trying to say I been in this house too long without bringing anything back. They are getting too hot and sweaty outside, and they need me.

They be talking. All day, Mama and Papa. Papa and Mama. They sit up next to that fence, and they talk.

I better go to the front door to let them know I'm still coming. I fill the frame of the door with my width and my height. I sign with my left and right index fingers and thumbs to make a square like ice. Then to make sure they understand me, I fan myself.

Mama lays the newspaper out across the table like the good cloth, the one in the closet we take out for company. I forget what it looks like. But I remember the way Mama treats it, soft with her fingers. She pets it with one hand and she supports it with the other. She carries it out like a tray that holds something small and once living.

Before she can spread out the newspaper, she clears the table with the side of her arm and her elbow. She pushes back the sugar bowl, her breakfast plate, and the hot stuff that stays out for Papa to brag to us about Louisiana. We have the only state in the union that produces genuine hot sauce. Papa says the peppers are pickled and bottled all near here, in a place where the Gulf opens up for the River.

This time of morning is still fresh, when Mama rises and reads me the newspaper. The shades are still drawn from last night, and cool hangs down like drops of water from plaster places cracked on the walls and the ceiling. Later, they will be all dried up. That's when Mama takes her midday nap and I do the first dishes.

But now the radio's playing sad and love songs. And it's too early to turn the game shows on tv. The good one comes on in the afternoon. You guess the words by the way the people act out what they want to say. I am better at that than the movie stars. I do it all the time. They just do it for a week or $25,000.

"Peanuts," Mama calls it. We both laugh because even though we are smarter, we know nothing about $25,000. We know a lot more about peanuts.

Mama reads aloud from the police reports, "There was a person speeding on Interstate 10. He was a Caucasian male, brown hair, blue eyes, and 35 years of age. He was stopped and interrogated by the police. But when he stepped out of the car, he was wearing no pants." Mama laughs. But I feel sad for him.

It is sad not to have pants at 12, 0, 0 in the day. That means noon. He must have been sticking to the seat of the car, with the plastic covers just squeezing his skin all around him. And he was driving alone with nobody to splash him with water and cool him off. Mama says, "Should have called the firemen better than the police." So maybe she did feel sorry and understand. But then she laughs again. I think she has a cruel streak.

Like when little cousin brought over her newest baby, Mama smiled at it. But when they left, Mama made fun of it to me.

"Look like a Chinese monkey," Mama explained because it was so flat face and black eye and bald. I have never seen monkeys except in the zoo one time when little cousin took me. I like the monkeys.

Little cousin had said, "Never in all your life you ain't seen a monkey?" I shook my head no, except on television and then they were kind of tiny-striped greyish blue. It makes me wonder if little cousin went tempted the face of the monkey upon herself by us stopping that day and staying so long at the cage. I feel sorry for the way her baby looks, except that the worst it looks in this life, the prettier chance it will have in the next.

It is Mama who only like babies and monkeys and Chinese in the next life, except if they begging. Then she says, "Them poor, poor things." But if a Chinese came sit at our table like that, Plop, just walk through the front door and sit down, bringing his own begging plate with him, I don't think Mama would give him her toast and grits.

That is why I have not told Mama about the miracle I saw in the paper. Yesterday, a foreign baby was smiling at me. When I got the newspaper off of the porch, the pages fell open to the picture of the foreign children and I was expecting only sadness and blessedness to appear. But in all her raggedy clothes, the foreign baby was happy.

She was smiling right up at me and I smiled back at her. And for a while, in the morning quiet before anyone got up we smiled silently just to each other. Part of the miracle was that neither of us felt more lesser than the less. It felt good like God was all around us, both of us not so good off in this life, but none the worse at the moment. It showed me there is peace and joy of the temporal flesh, in the way of miracles that you get now and then when God wants it to happen, just like when the Blessed Mother appears in the rosebushes, or in the kitchen and bathroom windows of the people on Lapeyrouse Street.

Especially when nobody is expecting it, God ups and makes a miracle and you have to make sure you got clothes on or not doing anything that you wouldn't want to go down in the records of heaven. Or sometimes, if you been good, it catches you at just the right time. It was like that for me when the foreign baby gave me a smile. I have been trying hard, and wishing and hoping that this would happen.

I am not so crazy to think it was my own personal smile. It was in a newspaper for all to see. I am not crazy. Maybe I am

"Just A Little Slow." That's what Mama sings to the people who want to stare at me and ask me the same question two or three times. As if I didn't hear it. I'm not deaf. I can hear just fine. I'm not deaf. I'd shout it at them if I could sometimes for the words that they say over and over. It just takes me a minute to figure out how I 'm going to say to them what I need to say. I got to do my hands and my face just the right way for them to understand. And I'm still faster than the people on television.

But even Mama, she don't understand half the time. Still, it don't make no difference for what goes on goes on anyway. After breakfast, she climbs upstairs again to take her morning nap. She needs a beauty sleep, more, she says, than I will ever need it. Mama looks at her face in the mirror every morning before she goes back to sleep. "Look at these lines," she shows me the places where the sadness shows on her face. "Look at these veins," she shows me her legs, "And them poor old watery knees." Mama tells me her body is just a burden to her. It has been as long as I've known her. Mama says it's a curse to ever have been perfect and pretty. She says I should be happy she is now worse off than me.

When she comes downstairs again, I take her hand to go to the backyard to cheer her up. I show her the plants in the garden. The iris are as purple as the passion of Jesus, I want to say. But Mama moves on to the zinnias and daisies and yellow roses. She likes to pass her fingers over their stems to see if they have any thorns.

Once I put the thorns on my head like the halo wreath Jesus wore right before Easter. I came and showed Mama and Papa and company that we were having just at that moment. It was really quite beautiful, an accessory, like they call it on television when they mean a hat. I wove some of the roses into the crown so that they would match my dress.

"Halloo," Mama made like a cow sort of the way she bucked up fast out of her chair, mouth first coming after me. I think she wanted to say What The Hell's Wrong With You, as she often does.

But the company was the parish priest, so she went to say Hallelujah before she rushed me out of the room.

Mama and Papa had a fight over her words after the priest went home to the rectory. That is the place where they have only men who are priests, and cooks and housekeepers to serve them. They can live "high on the hog," as Mama calls it, because they are officially and noticeably blessed. I would not mind cooking for priests, but Mama says there will be no going in and out of their house for me as long as she's living.

That day, we had to cut up my crown of thorns to get it out of my hair. It got stuck up there in between all of my natural knots. Just like the bubble gum did once. It is easier to get aloose from gum than thorns. With bubble gum, I just got the kitchen knife and cut off the parts of my hair where it tangled.

Mama cried for the way I looked after. But since I looked worse that I usually do, I felt better. It made me closer to the scourged and the ugly.

Mama says my appearance is her worst concern. That is one of the areas where I disagree. I disagree with words, the only ones that go with my mind—Da soft or Da louder. If I really don't like what she says, I go very loud, Da-Da-Da. Once she slapped me across the mouth.

I am learning to control my temper because of the foreign children and the blessings of God. I know it is working. I saw my first miracle, as I said, in the newspaper yesterday morning. I have a plan. It is a secret that I will reveal only when I am ready.

This is the plan: I will end the suffering of the foreign babies. And when they are all happy, I will be free to be happy, and everyone else will be too. Just like Jesus, I will be free for the sake of all the people and, in the process, I might even get famous.

I have already taken the first step. To satisfy the foreign children will not be easy. But I have been practicing. Every morning before my feet touch the wood floor I go "JesusMaryJoseph" so they know I mean business. Then, once I got their attention, all three of them, I think most powerful prayers to St. Jude and St. Joseph, on my knees, not even anymore lying in the bed. I wash myself very clean so I will be a temple of the Lord when I go to fix Mama's breakfast. I don't even bang the pots against the side of the metal stove, like I used to, to get her out of bed in the morning. I let her get up when she wants. It is amazing. She gets up at the same time she always did. I know my prayers are working.

I have a box on the side of the stove, in the crack where it doesn't reach tight with the cabinet. That is my special place where I save for starvation. Instead of eating my breakfast, my lunch and my dinner, I wrapped them up in a paper bag or in plastic that comes from the fruits and vegetables, like a neat package, a Care Package, like they say on the television. I wrap up all my rice, meat and even the gravy—in the plastic of course—and I put in the box for the foreign babies. I will send it to them through the mail when I am ready.

I got grits from one week already in my crack on side of the stove. I got pannee meat, French bread, and my favorite, gumbo. I put that in a special plastic cup with tissue on top so it wouldn't spill, the paper would soak up the overwet and when it gets to China, they just got to open their mouths wide and squeeze it.

I know my suffering is working because I feel holier. And also because I saw that miracle in the paper. How that little foreign child smiled! We smiled together for a long time, just like I did with little cousin's baby, until Mama came down for her breakfast. Then I folded the foreign child back into the newspaper in such a way so she would be able to look out. Then I put her in the crack near the stove with the food, so wherever she was she could dream of it and smell it, just like I dream of babies some nights when Mama and Papa use all their words for arguing.

I think they argue about my twin brother. It worries me sometimes, as it must Papa too, that Mama just won't let him out. That would solve everything as far as I see it. We could have a baby and she wouldn't have to eat so much or be fat. When they argue at night and I am sleeping or I suppose I am—because that is a confusing time, not knowing whether to be asleep or awake, or whether you are or you are not anyway—when they argue Papa yells, "You do not have to eat for two!" That's how I know she is hiding my twin still in her stomach and feeding him all day so that he will not be like the starving children. I tell Mama for her comforting, "Don't have to think of the whole world all the time. Just think about us."

But Mama wants to be the least in this house. So she does sacrificing. Even though it hurts her legs to sit for two hours in front of the television, she watches stories from noon to 4 p.m., and even though pork dinners make her feel sick, she encourages me, "Loutie, go run in the Frigidaire and put me little salt meat in the beans."

I know she is thinking first of others because she told me, "Selfishness is a sin." She reminded me the last breakfast. I had acted out that she didn't need to eat for the starving children because I was going to send them my meals. But I can't always make myself understood. I did round with my hands and arm like a beach ball, then made sad with my eyes and fists like wiping away a tear, then I pointed my thumb to myself. I think she supposed I was telling her that I was sad because she was fat. And I meant that too. But I am sad for my brother who might never get out and who is putting in too much time being trapped in her stomach.

I wanted to tell her where babies are concerned, one more won't hurt the world, especially since God already promised him to us. Plus, if I get the food to one foreign baby so that it will not be so bad off, then we can get our baby because the starvation level would be evened off.

Papa asks what is wrong with me.

He stands over my bed where I'm laying and sleeping and dreaming about babies and he says, "It's not like you to be lazy, Loutie."

"It's not like you to be lazy," he repeats just like I haven't heard. But I heard him and I want to tell him but it seems like too much effort. Not that he would understand. He never understands when I sign in the language that I made up better than television game shows. He laughs when the people make their movements and try to guess the words all the time while he's watching. But with me, he stares confused and serious. Then quickly he turns away. It's like if he understood me, he'd have to understand me all of the time. But he's too busy for that. He's got fishing on Fridays. Saturday he plays cards, and Sunday is his day of rest. He showed me that once, written in the Bible.

"There is a difference between man and woman," he told me that day when I showed him I wanted to rest on Sunday too. Instead of doing the dishes, I stood over the sink with the Bible and when Mama and he understood I was like reading it, then, I took it with me and laid down. I did just like I saw the vegetable man's mule did once. It laid down there right in the middle of the street. Of course, it didn't have no Bible to back it up. I was protected, I figured. Papa came over to the sofa, and I handed him the Bible and pointed him out to a line.

But then he quoted to me, "Man may work from sun to sun, but woman's work is never done," and he showed me the place in the Good Book where God wrote it.

I felt very bad in those days, and I was mad at God. I did not know why God did not make me a man. Because women could have babies, Mama told me in consolation. But it seemed to me she was trying to be a man herself lately the way she sat around doing nothing. I supposed after she had me, then she could sit.

"I did my part, for 48 hours of labor and I raised you and it wasn't no picnic," she told me once. "Now it's time for you to do all the work."

Papa slapped her. I saw it with my own eyes. And he said she could never talk that way to me no more. And she sat down. But she never got up again to do a lick at a snake, as far as I could tell. I been doing everything around this house since that argument.

Papa don't make her do anything or slap her no more. But he also don't be around, except when they sit on the bench outside close together. Why they sit so close and argue so hard I don't know. I think it's so as he can remind her that he is the man, so she won't be the man and give him competition.

I think it's because she don't want any more babies and babies like I was that she won't let go of the twin. That's why maybe we could get one imported like from those foreign countries, a swap back if we could promise them there is more food where this came from.

I have been saving my food for two weeks now. And I meant to send it a week at a time. But there is a problem I never thought of. I got to get the mailing address and get someone to write it out for me. That is why it is taking so long. I handed Papa the newspaper. But he saw the smiling child and just smiled back at me. I pointed to the letters where they might say to mail, but he had turned away by that time. "I wish they would send us some money" was all that he whispered.

I am feeling weaker and dreamier. I see babies almost every time I sit down. Babies traveling on roller skates. Babies diving off cliffs. Babies doing the backstroke from Africa, India, China and Mexico to Louisiana.

Papa's got big hands on the inside the color of basketballs and lined like the giant webs of spiders that he waves in front of my face when the doctor comes. They are discussing the problem that has made me not want to eat. But they don't realize I am not eating for a good reason. It doesn't taste anymore. I can understand why the starving children get so skinny. If you don't have food, too much food makes you want to be sick. It makes you like having starvation.

I don't know what Mama is doing with the food she is saving off me not eating anything. I think she is devouring it up for it not to go to waste. That means she is now eating for three. As soon as I can I will have to begin saving again for the foreign children. Mama found the pile on side the stove and threw the food away. I heard her telling Papa, she don't know what to do with me and she never did.

It's not the first time she's said that. She says that to him quite often when I am sick and in hearing distance, or when I am angry and pretending I've left to the back of the house. I hope they don't do to me what they did to the cat. When the car ran over the cat's tail, it looked so terrible, Mama said, dragging its rear behind him, that Mama convinced Papa to put the cat in a bag and throw it into Lake Pontchartrain. I know how to swim, but you can't get very far once the sack gets wet and clinging around you.

If we had a new baby, I could be like Mama. I would teach it what to do, then, I would sit around like a man. I would say, "Baby, pick up those clothes in the front room," "Baby, get me some grits for breakfast." Except, I would be nicer and I'd let the baby be slower because she would not know the language.

When Mama found the food by the stove and the picture in the newspaper, she asked me, "Loutie, are you losing your mind?" My arms were too tired to reach up and tell her what I wanted to mean. So I just laid there looking up into her face. For the first time, she said nothing back to me. I mean, she talked like me. She shook her head from side to side, and she shrugged her shoulders up and pressed up the air with her palms.

I smiled then because I knew what she meant. And she smiled back at me. That was nice. Like another one of God's miracles come true. Mama never smiled my way before. God has been on my mind a lot lately with his wondrous works. I would like him to work my twin brother alive right now. Since Mama threw away my food for the starving children, I don't know if I will have the chance to make up another Care package and have time for them to eat up and then come join me.

Mama and Papa and the doctor are standing on side of the bed. All together they look like the monkeys—can't hear, can't talk and can't see. I could guess that Mama would go swinging around the room by her tail if she could, screeching and crying like they do when their cage is disturbed. But she never was one to say when something is really bothering her. She got pride, she always says. So most of the time, she just sits and, a little bit more than usual, she eats.

Papa don't say too much either. He just takes his big hands together and pushes them one against the other until the palms of them sweat, and he has to run them down the legs of his pants.

"Loutie. Loutie," Mama calls to me over my head. "Loutie, you going to have to eat. We got sweet potatoes, bread pudding, soup, gumbo, baked macaroni, smothered chicken, little green peas. . . . ." She goes on and on. The idea of it all makes me sick.

I begin to look at her belly. All the time she is talking, it is wiggling up and down with her deep breaths as she stands on side of the bed. It seems like a big hard head is inside. It makes a big basketball shape so solidly under her dress. I'll bet the twin is right there still working on this morning's breakfast.

I am starting to think that God loves the poor children much more, and He provides for them better. They got a guaranteed spot up in heaven while the rest of us got to work at being the least. I wonder why God makes it like that, for us to reach His goodness. It seems that He could love me just as much as the foreigners, if He wanted to be fair. And why doesn't He let my brother out? It has been more than 30 years since he has been in there. And it occurs to me that maybe I have to do something to rush this miracle along, like I did to get the starving child to smile in the newspaper. I think that I may have to get my twin out of there myself. Then all God will have to do is make the twin living and breathing.

Mama was mad at me after she found all the food. She sat at the table downstairs within my hearing distance and talked and cursed aloud to herself all morning. I tried to explain to her but I was upstairs and she couldn't see me. And Papa never understands when I have something important to say. I don't think words work ever or even to make them understand one another.

Perhaps I should eat a little just to have strength enough to show them how I feel. I want them to know I am going to save my brother from living his life in Mama's belly. If he don't come out and be baptized, he might never get to heaven. As soon as I get out of this bed, I am going to give him salvation. I am going to get the knife and cut him out.

Mama has gone to the hospital. Papa says it's her heart. He says that my being sick was too much for her. Plus, she got trembly when she saw the butcher knife. Papa says she is just tired because she had to cook and clean and do the things I usually do. I think she read my mind and went to the hospital to finally let my twin brother out.

I wonder if he will be tall as me, seeing how he is old as I am. Or if he will be just like a baby, like little cousin's, kind of crinkly and fat. I hope he doesn't smell. All of the strangest of odors came from little cousin's baby, sweet like the powder she put on his neck and the shampoo I use, and then sour like the food that Mama said was spoiled next to the stove. I wonder if his daddy is a foreigner.

Mama got mad and asked me, "Loutie, why you saving all that food for?"

"She think food is to waste," I heard her turn round and tell Papa. Him too, he shrugged, like the mute and the people on game shows. You would think he would understand me better coming close to my language as that.

I tried to tell them that the least of the least, they need our help. And food is what they have lacking. Even the priest said that Jesus, He fed all the people and had some left over. If Jesus could save food from sermon to sermon, it seems that so could we.

Besides Mama would not be going into the hospital to have my twin brother, except that I prayed, and sacrificed my nourishment, so that he may live. God likes to give miracles when we ask for them. Isn't that what prayer is all about?

"Ain't I done enough," she told Papa. "Loutie lazy around here is the last straw."

Papa said to her, "You the one made all her problems."

"You the one got me that way I never wanted," she said.

"You the one," he said, "made me sin."

"I would like to forget," Mama said, "Loutie ever happened. I wanted a different life."

But I didn't want them to forget me, so I ran into their room. God made me for a special reason.

I pointed both thumbs at my chest, in the center at my heart. Then I pointed my right index finger at Mama and the other at Papa. Papa held his face tight like he couldn't talk anymore. His words disappeared into air when he tried to begin again. And Mama covered her mouth with her hand. There were no tears in her eyes. She just looked at Papa and me, and said "I can't even think about it anymore. It feels like damnation." Then I got the butcher knife out of my pocket, and she took with her heart attack.

"When I die, Loutie," she told me once, "I want a big funeral." She handed me a piece of paper that looked like the grocery list. She pointed to the names, "I want Uncle Alvin, Aunt Marie, Soeur Tenise, and the nuns from the Holy Family convent to be sitting right up front. I want the priest from the Little Flower of Jesus shrine to say the words over the casket. And I don't want too many carnations. But I do want a band. Then you and Papa can walk slow behind the casket when the trumpet plays *Down By The Riverside*. Wouldn't you enjoy that?"

I tried to smile big for Mama then because this was important to her, I could see. But I really don't want her to die. As long as she lives, whether she knows it or not, I am leaser than her. I am always her child. Still, she's been here on earth for a longer time than we both expected. She planned for her funeral over 20 years ago. Since then, she's just been waiting.

Maybe she'll get her wish someday. But I hope it is not before I get a baby to keep me company. Papa can't understand a thing I try to tell him. He just knows talk. Mama always tells him that, "All talk. No action." To prove her wrong then, he usually leaves out the house. But it still comes off looking like no action to Mama and me, because what he does is no place where we can see it.

I want a baby so I can talk to it. Babies are all action and no talk just like me. "Babies take too much energy," Mama told little cousin to not bring her child around no more in her most polite way. "Childbirthing is a curse," she told me. But now Mama's going to get a baby herself from God, whether she likes it or not.

Papa and I don't sit too close on the bench by the fence. Sometimes, I think he's ashamed to be seen with me. "Loutie, can you go fetch me some water?" "Loutie is the clothes done out of the washing machine?" He's always asking me some question. I want to ask him when Mama is coming home. But he never understands me.

Mama came home skinny and weak and not talking. She gave my brother away to the hospital. Or either they drained him out of her when she wasn't looking. Papa said all kinds of strange wires, machines and plastic tubes came out of her stomach. I think they sucked my twin brother out into one of those test tubes and gave him to some lucky family. Lucky families like that are always on television. We don't have luck much for anything.

People say Mama's got a weak heart and it's no wonder. It hurts my heart to think that I'm not going to get my twin. Mama made me bring out her funeral list from the drawer, and she added some doctors to the bottom. "I think they'll enjoy it. Don't you, Loutie?" she managed to ask.

I think if we have any funeral it should be for my brother, who never was, never is and never shall be.

The foreign children are smiling in the paper almost every day now. They getting fed, I'll just bet, by other people. People who send them money. Or people who don't have fat mothers. Or people who sing on the television. I can't sing and I can't save food any more or Papa will catch me. And I can't do nothing except what I been doing before. But no more does it make me happy.

It is because I can't help the least of the least like Jesus asked me to do in His Holy Name. So now what is going to happen to me?

The foreign children really got it the best. They are blessed from being miserable right from birth, without any choice or temptation. The Bible warns that the body traps you in all around. There never would have been sin if it wasn't for too much eating.

But maybe Mama will really die this time. And after that Papa will die too. And then there will be only me. And I will be poor off then just like the foreign children. I will be orphan and thin, except I will be older and I will not be in the newspapers.

Alone, I will be the most least because no one will know how unhappy I am. I will sit down by myself in front of the radio, and I will say my prayers and even maybe practice starvation. I will go one day, two days, three days a week. Then two weeks. I will say "JesusMaryJoseph, take care of your poor creature."

And they will answer my prayers because they will know I finally have nothing and have never wanted nothing of this life save for the love of God. And then, the burdens of the flesh will be lifted up off of me.

Life Is for the Living

The graveyard is about the hottest place in New Orleans at noon in the summer. But Thomas was touched in the head, or "teched" as people explained with one word and the tap of an index finger against their skulls, because every day when the twelve o'clock whistle blew like an air raid warning over downtown and workers everywhere glanced up from their desks to their boss to the clock that he used to measure their time, all the men who lifted cargo at the railroad receiving dock finally sat, except Thomas, who walked over to the adjacent cemetery to have lunch.

Everyone, but Thomas, thought this was strange. Still, they excused it, knowing the way eccentrics flavored the city. Ella and Bella walked arm in arm, street after street, right hip, then left hip together throughout the community. A man called Father, Son, and Holy Ghost made the sign of the cross at every intersection. Everybody knew him and greeted him daily.

And Marie Laveau was queen of the city for two generations. No one bothered to discover whether it was Marie the First or, her daughter, Marie the Second, or the two combined, who called on spirits for more than 200 years. Plus, every other person downtown was some relative of the voodoo patroness, so her good intercessions were widely believed.

Consequently, people accepted Thomas' lack of normalcy. They excused his mathematical talk at the loading dock, equating the number of times they cursed a day to a word that would stretch like a train to Baton Rouge. They excused the pseudo-African costumes he wore every Friday specifically to parade his paycheck from the white boss' office.

(He dressed on those days in large, loose shirts made into Dashikis from fabrics with unpleasant colors and unseemly designs that could have made a dressing gown for somebody's sister—if she had a penchant for unnerving authority.)

They excused his sandals with socks, reviews of books on philosophy followed by tirades on basketball. They even apologized to each other for him.

"Thomas is just finding himself," said one of the men.

"He still has a young mind," said another.

They excused all except his sitting mid-day in the sun. Even the dogs knew better. They found a spot under somebody's front bushes or below a car, with the latter chosen carefully from those which had to re-park often.

Still, Thomas sat in the sun every day and got sweatier, but worse, smellier. So that by the time he returned from lunch, he reeked in a way that no man of science could find a chemical with which to compare it, if there was a man of science nearby. There were only the men of the loading dock and they were well versed in the smells of nature. So they said that Thomas smelled like bare feet taken out of leather shoes, like something that died, "like shit," and the outhouse, which most of them had visited on some excursion to the country.

Thomas had a unique and foul body odor. But he did not notice it.

Each day, after lunch, the boss sent Thomas to some individual task at the opposite loading station from his peers.

None of them wanted to take responsibility for telling Thomas outright just how much he disturbed them.

"Do you want to sit down with somebody who just finished lunch in the graveyard?" they asked each other.

Instead, sometimes in the morning, they joked aloud about the need for personal hygiene. They talked about sweat and deodorant. They spoke about the tourists getting the sunstroke and going crazy—permanently.

And Thomas agreed. He was amiable. He just didn't believe that the conversation applied to him.

Thomas thought he was special since he got their attention most of the time. He could not distinguish their negative feelings from positive ones.

And in fact, they did not dislike him. Observing his clothes, dramatic conversations, and peculiar perspective was a high point in the day for many.

Thomas was the subject of dinner table conversation and mirth in many parts of the city. Some men rushed home after work to report to their wives, "You'll never guess what that fool did today."

In absentia, he also entertained the patrons at the local bars. "He had on some get up that he said came from the Coat De Voir— look liked it come from the De Mississippi Coast," the men laughed.

People appreciated Thomas. Still, about the deeper value of Thomas' antics, people suspended deliberation. Certainly, it would reflect badly on them if they found any affinity to him—and they too had a streak of real crazy down deep that could gush to the surface one day like an oil well.

And Thomas pictured himself in a much more positive light, simply waiting for the day when the seeds of his thoughts would produce blossoms. He knew that the trivia his mind retained would someday prove of worth to others.

He memorized the data of sporting events and great disasters. He was versed in aspects of geometry, astronomy, Louisiana's history and geology or the lack of it given his largely-unmapped, swampland state. He was a master of French euphemisms which he sprinkled in conversation throughout the day—"mes chers" meaning my friends, "la bas" meaning where something should be put, and "ma t'neg" or "boon coon" meaning companion. His facility with language demonstrated his ancestry.

Thomas bragged that he was cross-pollinated—a New Orleanian called in successive periods of history (and depending on the speaker)—a mulatto, quadroon, house nigger, and Creole. Now, he described himself as "simply a man like other men seeking the meaning of his existence."

His coworkers muffled their laughs when they heard this.

As for the population of Louisiana Creoles, now declining, Thomas created his own statistics. He ciphered—200 million white people in the United States, 29 million blacks, and 22 million Hispanics. Since Creoles were all of those, but allowing for half of the blacks, whites, and Hispanics to be something other than Creoles, Thomas calculated 126 million Creoles living in America, and he applauded their proliferation.

He imagined that to feed all these people would take one oyster loaf po-boy dressed with lettuce and tomato stretching from New Orleans via the Interstate-10 to Los Angeles. Or either the super-sandwich would go up the Illinois Central train line through St. Louis and on to Chicago, just as the most ambitious Creoles had done. But then, keeping the mayonnaise cool and the butter warm would especially present a problem. Thomas figured. Each person could bring hurricane lamps or Zippo lighters to toast their own section, at a cost of $3.78 or $1.25, and he would put the people holding the sandwich in alphabetical order, beginning with Aguillard, Aucoin, Bagneris, Barthé and ending with Zeno and Zeringue. Computers would be needed to measure out how far apart each person should stand.

The point of this sandwich was to make a statement about America and race. The U.S. was completely wrong in the decades when it tried to force blacks and whites together. True integration could be demonstrated by the Creoles showing the unity of all races and human appetites when holding the French bread, Spanish onions, Italian Salami, German mustard, Creole tomatoes and Louisiana hot sauce.

People said Thomas was legitimately insane.

Others whispered, "He missed the boat."

Thomas, however, never heard them. And even in the graveyard, where he wished to hear voices, there was nothing.

He sat every day around the headstones provided by important, former funeral home directors Labat and Llopis, Gerdes, Geddes and Willis, and, of course, Charbonnet. He talked to them about history, the arts and sciences, but got no response.

Sometimes Thomas stood and lectured them, presiding over three-story white crypts, broken marble walks, and white-washed gravel and oyster shell lanes in the blinding brightness at mid-day. Thomas was the only moveable figure in a menagerie of headstones depicting a variety of occupations and avocations—a veteran cavalryman on a horse, a fallen deer, a departed orator.

Other times, he just sat, deep in thought. He told the men at work that the graveyard was a good place to meditate.

They did respect prayer.

Who in New Orleans had not said some novena, climbed up some church steps on their knees, taken home in a bottle some holy water or bones and dirt in a cloth—and it had worked just as expected? Not one of the men at the loading dock or even in all of downtown New Orleans was exempt. They believed anything was possible, so often, that the miraculous was ordinary.

Thomas was not that far off the mark on the folding rulers of the devout. His biggest problem was that he wanted to distinguish himself.

It helped that he wore strange clothes and sat in the graveyard. Still, he wanted these actions to be symbolic of his larger purpose. He wanted to be a leader although even he realized the irony: He couldn't be unique if he wanted to lead because then other people would imitate him.

So Thomas' new issue for contemplation was how to become famous, yet anonymous. He studied intensely.

He finally found the answer in *The New York Times*. He read a story about young men in that city who painted slogans on the subways. They were becoming famous but nobody knew exactly who they were.

The solution was graffiti.

Thomas imagined the stir in New Orleans where graffiti was largely unknown as an art. He discounted the scribbling on the projects' walls by kids who wrote phrases such as "Chillin Killin," "Find on Cloud Nine," and "Jo-Jo Heaven Mary." They couldn't spell much less have higher meaning. Besides, these graffiti writers confined themselves to the environments of the poor—the courtyards of public housing and the corners of the ghettos. They foisted blight on their own communities, urban pollution that would be fixed better with a fresh coat of paint than their meaningless incantations.

The New York Times told Thomas that artists of a high caliber practiced graffiti as sophisticated communication. He, for example, would root his poetry in the hieroglyphics of Egypt.

He took aim at one of New Orleans' highest leaders—the mayor.

Thomas snuck out late one night to write the first saying on the outside of City Hall. By the next morning, he had vindicated all the politicians who criticized the fiscal waste and the personal gluttony of the plump, self-indulgent mayor.

"HOG, HEAD CHEESE?" Thomas' graffiti asked. The round, pig-like letters made a great backdrop for the television station's announcer who walked past each colorful word in her broadcast.

Thomas' second slogan, criticizing a growing anti-intellectual sentiment of the people was widely misunderstood.

"ET TWO BRUTES?" he wrote on a French Quarter building. He didn't know it was a place where men met other men.

The conservative paper said in the headline "Sodomy Moves Outside" while the liberal weekly wrote, "Graffiti Slanders Gays."

The criticism that Thomas was prejudiced bothered him. So he wrote his third entry, "I AM A MAN." This totally confused everyone. They fought over whether he was gay or whether he was a member of the old Civil Rights movement. Some Hollywood people in town to make a movie protested that he had taken the quote from their film, *Elephant Man*, and infringed its copyright.

The newspapers buzzed with controversy.

Unaware of Thomas' messages, his neighbors said to one another at night when they peeked through the curtains and saw him sneaking into his house with a big satchel in the moonlight, "He just need a wife."

By their standards he was still a good catch. He was only in his 40s. He owned his house and had two years of college. He had beaten the odds by not going to jail or Jacksonville, the one word that named both the Louisiana asylum and its cherished hometown.

In fact, Thomas was in school while his coworkers were absent from the calm routines of education. They had battled addictions and had served in the military or both. They recovered clinging to life, and suspicious and fearing of the wide, open-ended questions that Thomas posed.

Thomas neither protested nor supported their wars. His inquiries were deeper, he thought, than the actions of bureaucracies and even men.

Still, they had answered the questions of their existence to their satisfaction by being able to wake up every morning while Thomas floundered with his questions unsolved and not one philosophy but dozens of conflicting explanations for everything.

That is, until everyone began talking about his graffiti. He began to have a purpose. But he also felt pressure: What did he believe? About whom did he feel strongly?

As for the graffiti, all the men on the loading dock had opinions.

"I wish I get my hands on that know-it-all."

"It take all kind."

"I hope everybody don't start doing it."

The more Thomas heard talk about himself, the more he felt invaded and unsure.

Now, more than ever, he looked forward to noon in the graveyard. And he tried harder to communicate with the spirits and ask them for inspiration.

But the spirits remained unwilling to communicate, and he waited longer and longer. He sweated more and returned from the graveyard reeking.

Finally, on his own, he came to a conclusion about his next public statement and what it concerned. Life itself was the obvious subject.

He would define himself and his relationship to the world and he'd also explain man and the meaning of existence—all in one word. One word for the world, he thought.

Thomas was transfixed by the possibility. This would be his most important contribution. This word would not only define him, it would make him.

He could put the word in some place high, like the International Trade Mart Building at the foot of Canal Street. He could write it in huge letters, or maybe he could even sky-write it. But then, first he would have to learn how to fly. This would take preparation. But Thomas, at last, had a singular purpose: One word for the world.

Thomas bought a little black and white marbled composition book. He wrote in it every moment he was alone, which, now, was most of the time. When he sat in the graveyard for lunch, he would plan the place he would write the word, the way he would write the word, and the reason he would write the word. He thought, long in the future, after he was dead, his biographers would study these notes.

Thomas began to write his own history, the feelings he had each day, his quotations about life and the reasons he felt neglected. The notebook got fatter. Thomas copied phrases from books in the library that discussed people in Louisiana, the French, Spanish, Native Americans, Creoles and Africans. There was more information in one place, in Thomas' notebook, about Louisiana culture than in any single source in the metropolitan reference catalog. His notebook became thick and misshapen with documentation and with his sweat on the pages as he wrote in the noon-day heat.

He did not tell anyone about this effort. It was his secret as the graffiti had been. He would offer his one word, then, they would become enlightened.

People wanted thoughts to be simple, words to be easy, "like the *Times-Picayune* cartoons," Thomas wrote in his diary of preparations. He researched the media. People enjoyed the platitudes that life went better with Coke, that clothes made the man, that survival was work, sex was love, and, especially, that people of color were minorities.

He asked the men at his job what they thought about life, and why they got up in the morning.

"If I don't get here on time, they dock my paycheck," one said.

"The baby wake me up before I'm ready," said another.

"I like to eat breakfast," said a third.

Thomas was baffled and shocked. How could they define their existence so easily?

For a time, he even tried to see things their way. Thomas spent months making himself mundane. He dressed similarly to them every day for work in jeans, white t-shirts and boots. He talked only about topics he heard on television and the food he had for dinner.

Ironically, they wanted him around less because he had

abdicated his role in their community. For example, James was always willing to trade sandwiches. Carroll could be counted on when someone was sad to cheer him up with a sexual thought. Foster didn't mind working hard and would be at your side if you woke up tired, as long as you bought him a beer. Angus could stop the boss from checking up on everyone for a while by throwing a temper tantrum about the way his truck rarely worked.

When Thomas tried to be normal for the sake of his notebook and his research, and stopped being their entertainment, he made them nervous. Although he no longer had the offending smell, he was still banished to the opposite end of the loading platform.

In his jeans and t-shirt, but away from them, Thomas sat down and looked out at the horizon. To his left, was the St. Louis Cemetery No. 2, a small town of crumbling white edifices. To his right were the projects, half-empty with broken, square windows like missing teeth. Thomas looked again, from his left to his right, and then stood to look harder because he could not believe what he saw. He walked down to the train tracks directly in front of the loading dock so that he could look once more. To his left were the dead, to his right were the living. He was equidistant from both of them. Yet he got no wisdom from either.

He looked down the train tracks and saw they came to one point in the distance, although he knew that they ran eternally parallel. He could run their length, he could walk, he could ride, and he would never come to any conclusion, and neither would anyone else. Thomas realized, at some point a person just made a choice.

He could not write this in his notebook. In fact, he threw it with anger under the overhang of the railroad loading dock. He was so mad that his blood pressure in the summer heat began to go higher and higher. Thomas passed out. Then, it went higher and he died.

When the boss found Thomas at 5:15 p.m., it was because he did not punch out his time card. He was usually precise about money.

He was still on the railroad tracks, still clutching his head.

The smell of his sweat gave way to worse odors.

The train tracks had to be washed after Thomas' body was moved to the cemetery where his parents, grandparents, and everyone that he knew were interred.

After his body was taken away, the place where he died needed to be scrubbed. One of his co-workers, Brian, was sent to do the job.

Brian considered it a shame that anyone should die from heatstroke. It was so useless.

He began by hosing down the train tracks and then the surrounding area. The hard spray shot to places much farther than Brian could reach. In fact, it turned up the notebook that Thomas had tossed aside in anger. Brian recognized it and retrieved it. But he had never learned to read very well.

Brian was a religious man and had enjoyed Thomas for his particular contributions. So, in his memory, Brian wanted to do something sacred.

He took out the pencil that he used to mark the measurements on pieces of wood that he was told to saw, and he opened the notebook to a blank page and signed his name: X.

Then, he went to the last page of Thomas' writing. Brian could not decipher the sentence, but it said: The word for the world is____. Then, nothing was written.

So, Brian decided to put an O on the line for the paycheck that Thomas did not receive.

Brian also put an X in the dirt in the middle of two trestles where Thomas died, and Brian made a similar cross on his forehead, his lips, and his heart as he had learned in church. He said a short prayer—that Thomas could feel the appreciation that the men had for him, wherever he was.

And having done all that he could, Brian thanked God for this small opportunity to mourn his friend. Then, he flung the notebook into the darkness under the loading dock and went back to work.

What Went Missing

Achille's Jass

When his 16th notes began to scatter across the page like displaced kitchen ants, Achille Piron lifted his head, put down his black pencil and rubbed the back of his eyes with his fists. Then he finished getting ready for work.

He stood in the mirror. An old man appeared wearing a sleeveless undershirt. He could feel that the armholes were frayed. He took a damp facecloth and wiped the hangdog caramel-colored face of his grandfather. Black moles in exactly the same places. He ran the facecloth over the top of his head and his half-moon of gray hair.

He rolled a white handkerchief into the crown of his ship captain's hat before putting it on. Then, he set off in his white shirt and black trousers with his trumpet to the funeral of a distant friend. This was the only gig he could get in 1965.

People whispered that he couldn't play anymore. They were wrong. At first, he had just gotten particular about the attention span of his audiences.

"Can't you shut your trap?" he was famously quoted in the newspaper when he shouted at a patron in The Blue Room. Musicians all over town called to thank him. But none would take him up on the bandstand anymore.

Now, his bookings came like this one, the result of a death. They were frequent enough. Musicians, his age and younger, were dropping to the sidewalk in the broiling sun, found floating near their skiffs in the lake, and slipping off in their sleep like the final bars of a bassa nova.

With the music gone, their wives and kin finally appreciated their men. They called up Achille.

"Carry him home right, Mr. Piron," the most recent wife had said about her husband's funeral today. She knew there were only a few musicians alive who could capture a man's whole spirit—lay him out from birth to death, and even, respectfully, honor his foolish heart. Achille would have agreed for free. Thank goodness he didn't have to.

Before opening his front door, Achille glanced back at his sideboard. His pressure pills were safely in the drawer below the framed photo of Josephine Baker. She was half-nude and in a skirt of bananas. Signed her name on the picture "with love"—as she did for everyone. Nearby was a painting of a Parisian landscape with its rolling hills, winding road and thin, bare trees. Achille had accompanied his friend Peyton outside the city that day. He gave the painting to Achille "so you can write a song of our memories." He had the title, "Scene from Afar," but he still struggled over the tempo.

Peyton's ghost held Achille back. Sometimes Peyton's subjects were dark-skinned and wide-lipped. But then he edited their features and gave them expensive clothes to make them more "acceptable" to the critics. Peyton changed his name to Palmer when he got to Paris. The song Achille tried to write was just as elusive.

More tangible were the champagne-stained letters in the sideboard's cabinets. They also held books—Zola, de Maupassant,

Voltaire and Hugo—that Achille had bought for a few francs. When he wasn't practicing the trumpet, he spent hours reading in his bed by the window in the 18th arrondissement. Often he read aloud, accenting less with his old Louisiana patois and more with a new Parisian intonation. Then, he was not alone. But, he found out that his girl had been with two band members before him. She was a *High Society* girl.

That wasn't the only reason, but it was his impetus to return home. The first verse of his own song had ended.

As Achille descended through his door blinds to the top of his wooden box steps, his teenage neighbor called out, "Who dead, Mr. Lee?"

Achille looked up into the sun behind the boy's back, and there appeared to be two of him. "Lebeau. Blandin." Achille gave the boy the name of the deceased and the funeral home so that he could join the dance later. The information was hardly needed. All of his neighbors would hear the music floating over the streets. The crowd would gather in front of the church and drag their feet with the dirge to St. Louis #2.

The boy was sitting on the iron railing of his porch and, as Achille passed, he politely touched his index finger to the side of his hat in lieu of tipping it. The boy and his double nodded goodbye and their six-inch-Afros waved.

Achille wanted to be charitable, but his mind kept talking to him like a drum beat: A comb. A haircut. A comb.

Achille resented the inference—that if he emerged before noon with his bone that he was headed only to the graveyard. He could have been going to play a luncheon at one of the fancy hotels, or heading to the airport without suitcases because someone else would carry them later.

But not likely. Who was he fooling? In the small town of New Orleans, everyone knew about his slow demise. He could not get any billings now. Not in the big red letters of the movie house turned theater that shouted, Ashford and Simpson. Not even on soft beige posters with three-inch-tall block words that advertised "BLACK AND PROUD" dances at the Laborers Union Hall and the Municipal Auditorium. Nobody wanted to hear real music anymore. Couldn't hear it. Just wanted electric guitar and rhythms to shake their behinds. Anybody could do that.

Just having these thoughts, he knew, made him old. But he had tried to think differently.

He went one night to sit in for his young nephew. The audience was respectful when Achille played, but broke out when the drummer hit his solo. Then, the electric guitar began to scream like a cat on a barbeque. Achille's head hurt and his ears rang nonsense sounds in his brain all night. He could almost understand why some of the younger players shot up.

He arrived at the funeral just as the coffin was coming out of the church. Achille nodded to the other musicians and got in line behind the hearse.

There was a lone photographer who stood nearby and asked the musicians to pose for pictures. Some of the young ones turned their instruments in such a way that their images would frame up nice in the newspapers. More likely, they wouldn't make the news, just the tourist shops. Some guy would sell their pictures as postcards and line his pockets.

But it was an even swap. The young musicians appeared to know what they were doing with their horns and drums. But when they turned to the side, they lost the tune and were too slow to catch up properly. The postcard sellers would have beautiful photographs of mediocre musicians. Those were the just desserts of people who put seeing ahead of listening.

At the cemetery, Achille put down his horn for a minute while the minister prayed and the pallbearers raised the coffin onto the slab. Then, the band members surrounded the crypt and took up a resurrection beat. They now picked up *Just a Closer Walk with Thee* in a six-six like someone stepping on hot coals with bare feet. The dancers nearby let their bodies sprint.

When the people came to plant him, Achille wanted the repertoire of his youth. At the wake before the rosary, he'd have a little Debussy from one of the B Sharp music club students. They'd open with his cakewalk *Le Petit Nègre*. Then, he'd have them play a little Dédé to match it, showing that if he had not been so black and so held back in New Orleans, people would know his name too.

Then, as the mourners ate breakfast, Achille would specify that someone should sit out on the porch with a guitar. He would pick the strings lightly like the beginning of *Malaguena* then crescendo at the series of strums. That would show everyone that Achille was a serious man and not afraid of anyone. Then the guitarist should do a little soft Mexican folk music, similar to the kind Danny Barker played—light fingers on the frets with rhythms like a girl walking across the dance floor with a little bounce in her step. It reminded him of the way his girlfriend, with confidence, asked him to dance one night at the Economy Hall. She later became his wife.

From the house to the funeral parlor, Achille dreamed that someone would let out a good wail. It was, after all, the story of his life and of everyone's. They got born and then got buried. What the hell was the point? New Orleans. United States. Africa. Earth. None of it made sense. He wanted someone to wail just a little and shout, and maybe even fall out once or twice while the minister spoke.

It would be slow going to the cemetery, and sweet as ever with people remembering only his good points at that moment. *I'll Fly Away* would play so smooth and sincere that somebody would believe it. The weak-minded, the poor children just learning catechism, the old ladies—all might be apt to believe that God could fill their minds, their stomachs, and remove their wants and regrets.

The music would be so convincing that the poor in spirit would let everyone see their tears and their faith for once. And they would convince others that God could relieve unending sorrow.

Achille knew he'd be flying overhead then. He could picture it now as he walked with the band at Lebeau's funeral, and they went into a 4/4 step of *Didn't He Ramble*. One, two, three, four. One, two, three, four. He felt as if he could march with his knees to his chest on that song. And he did in his mind. He felt lifted up to the panorama of his existence. Below him were his neighbors and relatives in their church clothes—men dressed in wilting wool suits, ladies in sheath dresses too tight around the waist and the hips. Behind them were the last of the real Creoles—good-postured middle-aged people in peachy skin colors, or sallow from hair tips to pink lips, or smooth chocolate brown. They eased along at the edges of the crowd to get in a dance step as moved by the spirit. They didn't jump into the group of hangers-on right behind the band because the Creoles had to keep up the appearance that they were dignified. Achille watched them as he circled over the crowd like a wide-winged bird.

The music came in soft gusts pushing him higher into the sky and low over the corners where teenagers threw craps, nuns waited at bus stops and lonely men stood on loading docks, trying to find meaning in their labors. Achille's song was their song. Because of his age, he could play loneliness better than ever.

His wife had died. His children had moved to California. Why couldn't he leave, they asked him. Nothing's going on in New Orleans, they said.

"Not without me," he answered.

After he returned from Paris, Achille tried to write lyrics. He wrote them in French. "Ton coeur souriras de moi." He told his girlfriend that it said, "Your heart smiles at me."

"Nice. But nobody will understand that," she answered him.

That day, he gave up on words.

Certainly French ones. And later English ones too. And then the girl.

She married happily to a bookkeeper.

But there didn't seem to be words for everything he felt. Only pure music made him fly. Around the neighborhood, through the hearts of his friends, into the graves with the dead, into the minds of the living. When he saw people laughing and crying at the same time, then he knew he had gotten the right tone.

The drum gave a loud, one two count, saying "Yes. Now." They were moving to the last chorus.

On tour once, Achille met a guy from Russia. Everything he said sounded like grumble, grumble, grumble.

"Can't you be more cheerful," one of the Dixieland players had said. He was wearing a plaid suit coat and a rebel flag under the jacket. His musicians refused to stay in the same hotel as Achille's band.

That night, he played for the Russian the instrumental of *Do You Know What It Means to Miss New Orleans?* and when Achille got to the chorus for the second time in the slowest 2/2 possible, the man wept. At the end of the song, the Russian wrapped his heavy coat around himself, shook Achille's hand and left. In a few days, Achille got a letter and inside was a piece of red fabric with a corner of yellow. "It's a piece of the Russian star," one his band members informed him.

A person had to know a little about life to understand music. Achille blew now as if he were playing his own funeral. He wove his story into the men around him who played theirs—wife left, truck broke, pregnant teenager, new house, fishing on the lakeshore. Redemption for Achille, he blew. Achille going through the clouds. He zipped up the scale, zipped up higher and held.

He ended it with empty lungs. The breath going out of him was a struggle, but his last inhale felt right, peaceful, and necessary.

The musicians nodded goodbye to the deceased's kin, shook hands with one another, and hugged goodbye. Someone offered Achille a ride home. He was sweating and sitting on the edge of a raised bier.

"I'm not far." He shook his head no. "I'll get there soon enough."

Soon he was the only one left in the cemetery besides the gravediggers. He watched them efficiently remove the flowers off the casket and slide it into the crypt. He was transfixed still when someone tapped him on the shoulder.

It was the neighbor boy with his hair undulating. The boy's friend stood a few paces behind in his shadow. Achille's neighbor was soaking wet from dancing in the second line with the mourners behind the band the whole time.

"I didn't see you there," Achille admitted. He was a little embarrassed.

"I hear you man," the boy's friend responded.

And in those four words, Achille heard the sound he sought most of all.

Achille closed his eyes and lay down.

The boy leaned over Achille and called "Help" with a dissonant squawk.

But the friend grasped both of Achille's hands and they rose into the clouds.

Seeing through Water

Sister Michael Patrick waited at the corner of Bayou Road for the Broad bus to Canal Street, and she sweated the whole hot time. She soaked through the layers of her long black habit, and, every few minutes, she pulled a white, man's handkerchief from its hiding place under the cuff of her sleeve. With the cloth, she patted her skin—which was quickly becoming rashy and red—near the hard, starched edges of her white coif. After 20 minutes, the handkerchief too was wet and heavy, and the bus finally arrived.

Sister pulled on the handrails and mounted the first, high step, then launched herself onto the bus. She took an empty seat in the front, but the window was jammed. Not just her pride forced her to stay in her place with the closed window as the sweltering bus jutted up the street. The virtues of faith and self-sacrifice kept her glued to her seat while she alternately felt faint and nauseous.

Through the window, Sister examined the native people of New Orleans. Their various states of dress showed the ways that they had adapted to the climate.

The children wore hardly more than underwear and were always barefoot. Their grandmothers wore big, flowered muumuus that let in the air. The young women, about Sister's age, had billowy, cotton shirtwaist dresses that showed off their hourglass figures. The housewives, standing in open doorways as the bus sped by, exhibited themselves in cotton dusters, often transparent, which differed little from Sister's nightgown.

And the men, who boarded the bus for work and whom Sister hardly dared to examine, wore work pants slung around their hips and undershirts that draped over their strong torsos. They hooked their index fingers in the collars of their laundered white shirts to carry them behind their backs or held them starched, clean and folded over their arms as precious as a maniple as they traveled to their jobs in the kitchens of restaurants.

Closer to the center of town, people walked with opened umbrellas to keep the sun at bay. In the neighborhoods nearer to uptown, far away from where Sister Michael Patrick worked, the women called the umbrellas parasols. Uptown was where the privileged and, not incidentally, white people lived. They were across from Canal Street, a cherished, local paradox.

The canal had never existed. Still, the street operated as the city's main artery from the lake to the river. And streetcars as nostalgic as ocean liners disembarked passengers at the entrances to the grand department stores. Then, as they had since they had opened, whites entered through the front doors, and colored through the back. It was now 1956, so an Irish missionary like Sister could enter through whichever door she desired.

She chose the door by her mood. Worn out sometimes from working in the Negro part of town, she accepted her privilege and entered through the front while a good white gentleman held the door for her. Other days, she felt more solidarity with the people she served, and so she entered from the rear with humble acceptance.

Today, she hadn't thought much about her entrance, only

that she was headed to Krauss to buy some heavy muslin to put in the convent for drapes to keep away the sun.

All the sisters suffered through the New Orleans summers. Sister Michael Patrick was no exception. She was a girl from South Boston like many of her compatriots. If her own story of arrival was any different, she did not know. There were many memories that the nuns told no one. She alone knew that her father had turned and walked away when she revealed her plan to join the convent. His response was so different from the way he had danced her sister around when she said she was getting married.

But that was his way with Sister: sideways glances with a smirk on his face, spinning his finger around his ear when he saw her as a young girl walking around the house with her face buried in a book. And the night after the party, when her sister's boyfriend, drunk and full of himself, pushed Sister down on the bed, her father got enraged at her.

These thoughts passed quickly like the images of odd houses that fronted the streets where the bus passed—tall, white two-story frames over little blue stuccos. They were a snapshot, then a blur.

Her mother said her calling was a good thing.

"It's a vocation," she pronounced the syllables slowly to Sister's father.

"She's a lost soul, that one is," he replied. "Let her go. She might find herself."

Sister could have seen genuine tears in his eyes when she left his house for the last time, a thin girl with an overcoat and a suitcase, but her own eyes were full of water.

The bus stopped at Canal Street and the driver handed Sister a transfer to the Canal streetcar for the remainder of the half-mile trip, even though, as a nun, she hadn't paid. Sister thanked him and bowed slightly. When she got off the bus, she gave the transfer to an old woman standing in the heat waiting. Sister decided to walk the rest of the way.

She had joined the Blessed Sacrament nuns, because she read about the Wild West as a child and loved it. The Blessed Sacrament nuns were missionaries to the Colored and Indians. Sister studied the pictures of the Indians' wise elders under the peaceful big sky. She admired the Indian children, as beautiful as baby dolls with long, shiny black hair and big saucer eyes. Their pagan names were so melodic that she could imagine herself calling them secretly like pet names before they were baptized.

After the sprinkling, they would take on the names of the Catholic saints—Theresa of the Little Flower, Poor Clare, Catherine Fed by the Dove, or Hilary of Sacred Memory.

When she became a novice, Sister imagined that she would have a life so different from everyone in her family that their talk of the old country in Ireland would pale before her frontier adventure. Perhaps there was a bit of pride in that thought, but didn't she deserve it, after the way her family treated her?

If she was a brawler, or a drinker, or had married a rough man, her family would have given her support and, sometimes, compliments on her endurance. But because she was quiet and hardworking, because she did not fuss when the soda bread was all eaten before she had dinner, and because she took out the garbage when nobody else felt like chasing the rats, her family took advantage and they made fun of her.

Now, Sister paused in the shade of a tree. She was wet and dripping. The sweat was running down her legs and she had only gone two blocks. "Jesus perspired blood," she reminded herself. She started walking again, block by block getting closer to the store.

The Order had shocked Sister by sending her to the Negro mission in New Orleans rather than Santa Fe. At the time, she didn't believe it was possible.

She walked around the convent speechless although she was bursting with anger. Hadn't they promised her a good placement?

Didn't they know her interest in the West? She wasn't like Sister Precious Blood or Sister Crown of Thorns who were always mouthing some political slogan or another under their breath that she suspected they also used for meditations in place of their prayers.

But she had already taken her vows of poverty and obedience. So she put her head down, looked at the floor, and said, "Yes," when Mother asked her if she was ready to go to the Deep South.

She read everything she could find about Negroes: the violent *Native Son*, the dramatic *Black Like Me*, and the tragic *Cry the Beloved Country*.

But when she arrived, she found the reality much different.

The Negro children were constantly making noise. Dancing around. Yelling and laughing. And the heat. The heat stretched from March until November and then broke only intermittently. In the heat, the children were more animated. Needing to go to the bathroom. Tugging at their shirt collars and pulling the shirt tails of their friends. Wrenching at her sleeves. Last year there was one boy in particular who seemed to be always in the back corner of her habit in her blind spot. Every time she turned, she tripped over him.

His name was Pierre Dorsay, his family apparently holding on to their remnant of French ancestry. Sister moved him from the front aisle of the first grade classroom where he kept coming up to her desk, to the back where he kept falling out of his desk to the floor. She moved him away from the windows where he kept staring out and pointing, to the opposite wall where he encouraged the rest of the class to stare out while he pointed for them.

She brought him to the principal who made him sit with her for a while in the big unpainted office. Then he was sent back to the class because he wore out the principal.

"Mr. Dorsay is your cross," Mother Superior said as explanation.

When she returned Pierre to Sister, he beamed. On another child, the look would have been beatific. But on him, it portended more misery.

And she couldn't admit to anyone the intense feelings he evoked in her, her powerlessness and ineffectiveness. And worse, her anger when she punished him, especially when he didn't respond. She gave him extra math work that he returned with missing pages. She sent notes to his grandmother, on which he engraved vulgar words and stick men. She kept him after school for chalk-cleaning sessions that exploded dust all over the room. At such times she found herself shouting at him, sometimes over the din of the laughter from the other miscreants. "Mr. Dorsay," she caught herself shouting, "Please, shut up and sit down!"

And in the fraction of a second before the sudden, stunned and frightened silence of the children, she would think of Pierre Dorsay as a messenger from Lucifer who deserved her criticism, "You are ignorant, and you deserve it." Thank God, she never let the words out.

Instead, she left the classroom to calm herself. The silence of the children was broken only by a few whispers behind her. And when she glanced back, she saw Mr. Dorsay circling his finger around his ear, leading the talk about her—crazy.

Finally, Mother Superior saw fit to place him in another classroom. That teacher broke the ruler across his hands. Sister heard that still didn't calm him.

Thankfully, now in the summer, she only encountered the children accompanied by their parents at church, and when they came to the convent, it was to help sweep, or clean windows, or dig in the garden.

Today, she had the pleasant chore of shopping, were it not for the sweltering heat.

In the cool summer of Boston she would have already taken down the damask of the winter and put up the summer sheers. Strange that, in Louisiana, the heavy curtains were used to keep the sun at bay.

The convent's parlor was kept dim so the room would stay cool. Only when a visitor entered did Sister flick on the lamp.

Once, she sat in an armchair opposite Pierre's grand-mother. They were on either side of the lamp, although only the grandmother sat in the circle of light. She questioned Sister Michael Patrick about taking Pierre out of the class and placing him somewhere else.

"Pierre say you the most nicest one," his grandmother explained her reasons for wanting him to stay put. "Why you can't keep him with you?"

The sides of her mouth had deep creases. Her cheekbones were hard cliffs of flesh.

"I can't seem to reach him," Sister said. She pictured him sinking in his desk. Her instructions floated above his head. "He needs more discipline," she added.

"I disciplining him all the time, Sister. You'll see. He be better," the grandmother said. "He do all his work and listen."

"I am sorry," Sister said. And she got up to open the curtains. The bright light shocked silence into the room. The heat entered in waves.

"Thank you, Sister. I know y'all tried," the grandmother said, rose from her seat and took out her white umbrella for the long, hot walk home.

"Don't worry," Sister told the grandmother.

But Sister knew Pierre would get no better.

By the time Sister got to Krauss to buy the fabric, the sky was getting dark as it did every afternoon. In a moment, the clouds, which had collected all the humidity of the morning, would break open. The rain would fall heavy and thick to the ground. The thunderstorm would last only about 20 minutes, but its force seemed endless and foreboding.

The first year she was in New Orleans, Sister was afraid the rain would continue all day and night, and at that pace, it would pile up four-feet high like the Boston snow. Then what would they do? Where would they go? Surrounded by the lake and river, water covering every street corner and coming into every classroom? Sister imagined that they would disappear off the face of the earth, all of them too insignificant to find.

On blustering overcast days in Boston, her own grammar school teacher put on the radio in the afternoon to allay students' fears while they put on their overcoats and boots to go home. The children glided to the closet on Mozart and daintily put on their mittens.

But when Sister turned on the radio in New Orleans during a thunderstorm, the classical music never sustained. Dixieland soon came on and Pierre took that opportunity to lead the class in a second line.

The first time he did this, Sister was confounded. On one particular note all the children jumped out of their seats, waving head scarves and handkerchiefs. Even the quiet ones began prancing around.

"May I have order, please!" she found herself shouting as she switched off the radio.

Pierre alone didn't hear her. He was leading the dance outside into the rain.

Now, Sister arrived in the cavernous fabric department of Krauss. Silk fabric covered long cardboard tubes against the wall. Madras plaids and printed flannels, and every type of brocade and cotton sat in rows of bolts. The high-ceilinged room produced a glorious empty presence.

The cloth muffled the voices of shop-girls whose accents came from Italy by way of the swamp.

"What you want, Sister?" a voice said. It had a rhythm like the chorus of the song *Steam Heat* that Sister remembered from childhood. The voice belonged to a woman with yellow hair sprayed into a narrow, vertical shape above her wide head. Her nod at Sister and the scissors in her hand indicated she wanted to help.

"Do you have a dark, heavy muslin?" Sister asked.

"Mae-king curtains?" the woman asked. Sister could hear the woman was being polite.

Then she turned and called across the aisles in her normal speaking voice, "Wanda, what you got here for Sister?"

"Some few things," she replied, "Send Sister over here."

Sister crossed to the other aisle.

She had been Sister for five years now. Before that in her house she was Maggie.

"Maggie-girl" her father called her when he was drunk.

She saw him tipsy every day, dancing and singing loudly over her mother who was trying to cook and discipline the children. He didn't notice when they all went to bed.

Only Sister now slept by herself.

She struggled to breathe often at night in the convent. Even under the open window, the air sat on her chest like a hot towel. When prayer didn't help, Sister flipped on her lamp and closed her eyes. She got comfort from watching tiny dark spots scuttle across the inside of her eyelids.

The natives of New Orleans put up shutters on their houses to keep them cool. Door shutters locked on the inside and had slats so that the light and air could be controlled. Down in the morning. Up in the afternoon. The light stayed apart from the shadows in distinct lines.

Except sometimes, when people didn't watch their blinds, the sun moved fast and the room was completely dark in the middle of the day. But that was fine for most New Orleanians. They only needed the light for a few things—sewing, ciphering, and nourishing their indoor plants. So they postponed their activities, preferring to sit in the dark rooms and be happy.

Sister's room was often over-bright and steamy because she fell asleep with the light on. She resolved that she would get enough fabric to make drapes for herself the next time she went to the store.

The day that she stood finally waiting for service in Krauss' cool fabric department, Sister heard a commotion in housewares. There were sounds of boxes falling into the aisle and glass smashing. There was a mass of fussing and hollering. The voices came loudly over the quiet floor to her.

She heard a thump. Then silence, and a man yelling "Gotcha."

She heard the voice of a child saying, "Leave me alone."

Sister's heart suddenly went heavy.

"I tell you," Wanda said to Sister, "some people don't know what to do with their children." Then Wanda added calmly without looking up from the fabric, "They come in here by themselves all the time."

The commotion was now just a few aisles over. A tall guard stood near someone who had his hands up just barely over the bolts of fabric. Long, brown fingers pointed to the sky. Big boned, skinny arms. Ashy elbows.

Sister stared at the nearby cotton. Her heart started pounding.

Then she heard more movement in the nearby aisle as the fabric swished. She turned back to see big bolts of silk being jostled down the row like boats in a harbor when a big ship pulls in.

"You see who it is too, huh?" Wanda now nodded her head in the direction of the noise as she faced Sister.

Sister now had to look.

"Who it is" was the New Orleans' way of saying "Negroes again." Many of the shop girls at Krauss objected to the owner's policy of allowing that population into the store.

Negroes came through the back door of the store too often with wide smiles on their faces even after they got a cold once-over from the security guard. Negroes shopped plentifully at Krauss, even asking sometimes for double bags.

"Me, I don't wait on them," Wanda continued her sentiment. "Her over there," she nodded now to the blonde, "She can't walk fast so she always gets stuck." Wanda had raised her voice so that the woman with the scissors heard her and chuckled.

Sister suddenly felt a little dizzy and nauseous.

"Excuse me." She headed for the ladies' room.

But she had to walk past the aisle near the commotion. She ducked her head between her shoulders and tried to glide by unnoticed.

The noise had quieted down as Sister approached. But then she heard a loud smack. It was the sound of skin hitting skin and bone. And she turned toward it.

She heard Pierre's grandmother's voice. It said, "Boy, ain't I told you stay next to me?"

Yet Sister heard no reply, nothing from him. No talking. No crying.

Instead, her own chest heaved, and nausea, fear, and sadness flooded her. She was drawn to the scene and continued to move closer, against her better judgment.

When she got there, through her watery eyes, she saw Pierre. His face lighted up.

His grandmother was commiserating with the white guard, who was nodding in agreement.

She said, "I be asking people, what you do with a child like that?"

The guard shook his head from side to side. He didn't seem to know either.

Pierre continued to look only at Sister as if he were not in the store at all. She had seen this stare in class. He was somewhere he could not be reached. Conversation didn't work. Neither did discipline or even Sister's frustration.

Sister did not try to look back at him. When she reached them, she did not say hello to Pierre, his grandmother, or the guard.

With her shaking hand, she grabbed for the boy. His palms, unlike his eyes, were wet and hot. Sister pulled him by the hand away from the group, her outstretched arm dragging him behind her, down the escalators and through the open front door of Krauss.

The rain had begun to fall on Canal Street and since it was not a true outlet to the river or the lake, there was nowhere for the water to go. It filled the gutters and puddled up to the sidewalks. It made little lakes where the tar in the streets had melted away and the shell-filler emerged.

People crowded together on the sidewalk near the outside wall of Krauss to stay dry. But Sister brought the boy into the downpour.

Pierre brightened like a wilted plant. He raised his arms and his face to the rain as Sister watched.

That's when she saw God's plan.

Pierre stood in the pose of the saints, the evangelicals and Sister herself the night she felt most alone and prayed in supplication for someone to love her.

Sister reached into her sleeve and brought out the white handkerchief and began waving it in the air as she had seen the children do when they danced the second line. Pierre became aware of her then, faced her, and shook his shoulders and hips. They circled around one another as the rain came down, and they continued to dance as the thunder crashed and the lightening lit up the sky.

The Beginning of the End

Behind the Catholic church, sharing a backyard fence with the rectory, is the one-man tabernacle of Mr. Henri Chapon. He is a knot on the loose branch of a famous Creole family in New Orleans. He is now broken away because of his stringent religious beliefs, among other things.

Another reason is because they don't acknowledge him. He is an embarrassment to all of those great-grandchildren bearing the Chapon name or physically favoring their ancestor with his high forehead and pointy chin.

Mr. Henri Chapon shares those physical attributes of the famous philanthropist and educator. But that is not so important. More relevant is that his "heart weeps for all the worldy world." He says this aloud to the mirror when planning his sermons from the front porch. He loves every soul, he adds—"Jew, Gentile, White, Hindoo, Indian, Negro, Black and Colored"—then he chuckles, "Ah huh-huh." But he is serious, his reflection knows. Chapon feels more related to every man than to his real family. Yet, from the latter, he reminds himself to no longer "seek ye praise or recognition." He prays for them.

In fact, Chapon planned to offer up petitions every Sunday, on the gallery facing Rocheblave Street of his one-man church, also known as his house. At first, neighbors passed around the word that by converting his house into a place of worship, Chapon wanted to dodge taxes or the law.

"What's the difference?" some asked. Neighbors gathered quickly to debate his finances on the sidewalk across the street. The night before, they had tried to look through his un-curtained side windows. He had just moved in and was declaring his calling aloud.

"Lord, I'm ready! Lord, I'm ready," he bellowed at intervals from the lit front room.

Chapon didn't realize he was so noisy until he saw a few faces peeking into his window.

Two days later, he put up a sign. It was a blank piece of whitewashed plywood that hung on a long piece of jump rope that he had found in his backyard.

That was his first miracle.

He was standing in the dark under a pecan tree and peering through the chain link fence to the windows of the rectory where the priests were eating dinner. When Chapon tried to walk closer to the fence, he tripped over a rope. He imagined it was a snake.

"Back Satan," Chapon hollered as he fell on top of hard lumps of unshelled pecans in the grass. He lay for a moment with his big belly pressed to the earth and his arms stretched over his head, as prostrate as a novitiate.

And as he thought about his position, Chapon understood faith was the only way for him to get up.

"Whoa Lord, take this trial away from me, if it be unnecessary," he prayed as he waited for the thing touching against his ankles to move up his legs. He whispered aloud, "Take the cup, Lord." He waited. Nothing happened. But something very important did transpire in Chapon's mind. Trembling, he reached down to touch the snake and behold, it became a rope.

"Ha-lay-lu-ya," he stood up and shouted at the priests' house. One of the youngest came to the window and Chapon shouted "Peace, priest!" in his direction. But the priests' housekeeper came and closed the window.

Chapon carried the rope with two hands over his head like Moses displaying his holy scepter. Later, Chapon tied the rope to both ends of the plywood sign and hung it over the porch entrance to share his miracle with the whole neighborhood.

The sign hung for a few more days like a big, square, white cloud. Children passing speculated that Chapon was going to open an ice cream shop or at least sell frozen cups so that they wouldn't have to walk two blocks away. The youngest children wished aloud the most since they were not allowed to cross the corners alone, and had to depend on their reluctant brothers and sisters to escort them.

But Chapon wanted to keep everyone in the neighborhood waiting. Hesitation always produced want. Then he began to prepare sermons, one for each of the four words he planned to paint on his sign, one word per week.

His neighbors were mostly curious because Chapon's reputation preceded him. A decade earlier, he was the notions salesman for their Seventh Ward neighborhood. Chapon slowly drove a wood-paneled station wagon up and down the neighborhood streets, parking it on every other corner and walking door to door to sell towels and sheets, cotton dresses and slippers, nylon underwear and cutlery. They were among the items that black people couldn't touch in the stores during segregation for fear of being tossed out, and they were still self-conscious of handling them in public.

The company had purchased Chapon's selections on whim at wholesale prices. The company's assistant vice-president—the president's daughter—was an impulse buyer and she recognized the same compulsions in everyone.

The uptown firm was quick to employ Chapon. He was very light-skinned, and he could work the Seventh Ward blocks where whites and blacks lived on alternate streets and hated each other over the backyard fences.

The white homeowners did not know that Chapon was a Negro or they would have never given him their money. The blacks knew, of course, because many of them had some relative who looked like Chapon, and they widely acknowledged the notorious sexual mores of their miscegenistic kin. The Seventh Ward Creoles were too proud to "go white" as did their other light-skinned relatives who passed and wed whites just across town.

These white Creoles saw the black Creoles as sentimentalists with not enough good sense to get ahead. The blacks saw the whites as opportunists who rejected all emotional attachments. But neither accused the other in public. That would have been disloyal to family, and un-Christian.

Chapon was both too emotional and too opportunistic: first, as a salesman and now as a minister.

But people hardly recognized the old Chapon. When he tried to buy groceries with a check (the last from his previous, material life), the clerk requested an ID.

"You're not Mr. Chapon," she said.

Chapon, then, raised his palms up to heaven and he clasped them like everyone's living room picture of the pale, praying hands. He concentrated on them alone as he stood in line and waited for a miracle.

"Lord, lift me above this confusion," he said.

People behind him in line laughed and shook their heads sadly. One angry woman pushed past him, "Don't I got enough trouble without running into these religious nuts?"

Chapon didn't hear her.

The store owner came over and approved Chapon's check, anxious to get him outside.

Chapon poured his canned goods into a sack that he got from the French Quarter in another miracle situation. He had been picking through rotten vegetables and food that spilled off carts and had been smashed by traffic, when he came upon a nest of rats. They were feeding off what appeared to be the inside of a cat. When Chapon came upon them, he stamped his foot and shouted, "Scatter Satan."

The rats ran. Chapon went to pray over the cat's carcass because of the sadness that one animal should feed on another. Chapon had given up meat. He went to pray for the soul of the poor, dearly departed cat, but when he got close, he saw it was pasta with meat and tomato sauce. "God delivers Daniel from the Lion's Den! Hallelujah," Chapon stamped his feet and sang.

The miracle of that night was so real to him, he thought of it frequently as he moved into his church. Actions could really change reality. The Baptists had singing. The Catholics had frankincense. The Rollers had dancing and rolling.

He got a new plan. Instead of preaching to the people in the Seventh Ward, he would act out his message.

Chapon began practicing in his living room. The first word of his message was the easiest. It was inspired by his favorite, Jesus on the cross. Until he got the nails, hammer and wood, he decided to do without props. Chapon stood in his living room and stretched his arms out on both sides. Then he put one bare foot on top of the other, and let his head drop. He did that for about three minutes. Then, he became tired. So he lay on the floor and did Jesus on the cross lying on his back.

Such was the image neighbors saw on the first Sunday of Chapon's passion plays. First, Chapon brought out a step ladder. He carried a small can of black paint that he put on the ladder's platform near the top step. Then he mounted and steadied the swinging sign with his left hand and painted with his right. He made the letter T, in a style just like out of the Bible. Then he dismounted to give the neighbors the lesson of the initial. He stood with his arms wide open like acting out the cross.

The children who were passing on their way from church rushed home. The older boys stood for a while, watched Chapon and discussed whether to pitch rocks at him.

Chapon was thrilled. They had recognized his similarity to the Lord. Which one would pitch the first stone?

But a woman called from her porch, "Don't you boys throw that or I'll get the police."

Chapon was grateful. He was happy enough that the Lord's deeds were acknowledged. He didn't want to get hit.

After a while, Chapon climbed the ladder again. He steadied the sign and added HE to the T.

"Jesus," Chapon addressed the scattered neighbors watching, "was a man." Then, he went inside.

Since he lived alone, Chapon could readily appreciate the sacrifices of the Lord. Chapon once had a wife and seven children. Sometimes he began to miss them, but the power of his faith took over. It quickly reminded him to let loose of the world. "Poverty of the flesh do feed the spirit," Chapon preached to himself in times of weakness. He left his family permanently for his calling. It was a necessity of his religious life.

The nuns stayed chaste. And so did the house full of priests across the fence. They chose to be celibate. Chapon would have denied his sexual life too, from the beginning, if the seminary had agreed to keep him. But he had refused to bring Communion to the convent. Too many females. Then, he had begun scratching his elbows raw. And when his superiors assigned him to counsel the girls from the nearby high school, he sat and listened to their problems while rubbing his sweaty palms against the legs of his pants until they were damp. The head priest who told Chapon goodbye assured him that more worldly experience would be good for him.

And Father was right, celibacy did not come naturally, as Chapon found out many children later. And even now, he speculated about the appearance of the woman who kept the boys from pitching rocks at him. Then, Chapon dismissed her quickly from his mind. "Thou shalt not commit adultery," Chapon preached to himself. Years earlier, he had used those same words with his wife. But she broke that commandment many times.

Chapon suddenly felt inspired. He returned bare-footed to his front porch and announced to his neighbors, "Jesus was a real man." Then, he turned around, walked into his house, and closed his front door with a slam.

Chapon broke into a sweat when he got inside the house. Or perhaps, he had a chill from the air conditioner. Outside was hot and he wore only a bed sheet wrapped around his waist and thrown once over the shoulder. He was soaked where the bed sheet was tucked around an old belt, which he had fastened by making a knot.

Chapon went to warm himself up with hot soup. He got a can of chicken noodle from the cabinet. He put the fire high. The temperature in the kitchen rose and condensation formed on the plaster ceiling. Drops of water fell on Chapon's bare shoulders and ran down his back. It gave him chills again, but of a different kind. Chapon felt pleasure—warming, chilling and eating the soup. He forgot his vow not to eat meat. It just slipped his mind.

Chapon had a dream about the way to act out the second word for his sign. The next Sunday, he scripted END in a flowery, old fashioned print that dripped only once when the sign swung backwards, as Chapon turned to see whether the woman across the street was watching. He came down the steps to the porch and tried to define finality for his motley, but mostly curious flock.

"You know when something's gone," he told the few neighbors who gathered.

"Who stole it?" asked one of them, eager to participate.

"No, I mean, gone and finished," Chapon said, "Like when Lot wife turned to stone because she looked at the Sodom Gomorrah. She was finished." Chapon stood up and pretended to be a statue with its back to the crowd. They held their breath for a moment as he stood motionless, afraid he might do something strange. "A Lot was gone," he explained when he returned to his seat on the step. "Like some things is just finished. Like when your son leave home for the army, he ain't no child no more. Or when you a old man, that's the end of your days Cassanoving." A few in the crowd gave an embarrassed giggle. "And some things is just the end by they very words. The end of the line. The end of your paycheck. The end of this sermon." He walked inside and closed the door. Chapon did not come out again until the next Sunday.

One reason he didn't come out was for good example, to show them the finality of the end. In that way, his sermon worked because people got to thinking. He'd left so abruptly, and they had many questions. They waited on the steps for him to come back. Finally, when he didn't return they dispersed. But they waited for a good 15 minutes.

Some concluded he was just crazy. A few went back to their porches across the street and sat waiting until the sun went down. They wondered what Chapon was trying to pull. They told the woman across the street what happened when she returned from mass. The old ladies speculated to her that maybe Chapon could make some miracle. Maybe they could see their own dead mothers and brothers one last time. Stranger things had been known to happen through the power of prayer.

The woman sat on her porch after dark. She found herself staring at Chapon's house. She even began worrying about Chapon after a few days. But she didn't dare ring his bell out of her shyness and his possibility of insanity. Still, she knew God did work in mysterious ways.

Once, she also had wanted to give her life to religion. She had wanted to be a nun. But she was not allowed. She was the surviving caretaker for an old aunt and uncle. The church had said she couldn't work any better for God than to take care of them. So she had dedicated her life to her elderly. But then, after they were gone and she wanted to live, she was too late for her goals. She wanted a family, but no man now looked at her. She had deserted fashion and femininity about 30 years previous. Now she had a slight mustache over her lips, and the pleated skirts she wore far below her knees showed dimpled, fleshy ankles.

Her calling had used her up. But that was the purpose, she consoled herself. Everything in life has a purpose, a beginning and an end.

Chapon was thinking a similar thought as he waited the week in his house. He was thinking about his next word IS, and how the word IS and the word END would just be up next to each other like that. One word expressed all finality and the other expressed all life. IS meant that life was eternal. IS meant that a full life was for everyone. IS was a word that had always confused him. He spent the week tossing and dreaming about the word IS.

Chapon did sneak out of his house a little to go into his backyard to see how other people spent their lives, their ISes. The priests said they spent their IS in service just to the Lord. But Chapon could hear them laughing and arguing in the evening. One night, they played cards. "Gin," one of them shouted from the kitchen table. "John, you are just too lucky," another replied. "Don't be a sore loser, just do the dishes," the winner admonished. The winner agreed to dry the dishes after the loser washed them.

Chapon thought of the time before he wore a sack or a bed sheet as his first IS. He dried the dishes for his wife. And on the nights she didn't come home, he cooked and cleaned the house too. Chapon put the children to bed, all seven. A lucky number, Chapon thought, until his wife began seeing another man. She had started coming home later and later from church. At least he thought that she was at mass in the evening. Then, he found out that she was seeing her most recent lover.

"Why can't you be satisfied with what you have here?" He fought with her.

"What do I have here but trouble?" she replied.

Chapon's first IS was a WAS now. But how could he explain to common folk that the Lord had made a way for him. His IS was now in the Lord's service. Suddenly he got inspired.

The next week, after he painted in a scrolling hand the word IS on his plywood sign, Chapon became very active in the IS of his neighborhood. Monday, he brought groceries to old Teresita on the corner, although she wouldn't open the door to let him inside. He left the groceries on the porch. On Tuesday, he bought freeze pops for the neighborhood children. They all came to his step, except one boy who came late. Chapon gave him a nickel.

By Wednesday at 5 p.m., several people were near his porch with looks on their faces that said they would take anything he handed out. He invited them all in for dinner. They ate butter beans and rice on broken china with mismatched cutlery. On Thursday, some of the housewives of the neighborhood came to demand, "What's going on?"

"This is the Lord's work," he said. He promised each of them to come to their houses and mop the floors. He promised to arrive on Friday to the few that said yes. He went to two houses. Both were adjacent to the woman across the street who had turned away the stone-throwers. Chapon found out that her name was Angie and he got inspired. He had done no good work for her. So he went over and rang her bell.

"I am here to do the Lord's work," he said.

"What can you do here?" she asked.

"I can see that you are lonely, Sister," Chapon replied.

He saw her eyes well with tears.

"Let me come over tomorrow and we will pray together."

Saturday night they knelt in her front room near the open door so as to be chaste. Chapon went home right after the prayer ended.

Sunday morning, Angie woke up happier than she had been in a long time. She knew this man was doing the work of the Lord. A man had not been in her house since her old uncle. And Chapon had prayed with her so earnestly that she found him attractive.

Chapon had matching thoughts. Since he left his wife, he hadn't been near a woman. Angie smelled good. It was pleasant in her company. The word NEAR struck him. The word NEAR was a sign from heaven. The Lord wanted them to be closer.

The Lord always had the answer that Chapon needed exactly when he needed it. Chapon thought of the great mystery of faith. The Lord provided for the birds of the air, the chosen people, the priests and the nuns who had taken vows of poverty and chastity, and for all the people of the Seventh Ward. He seemed to give the Creoles great faith or good looks when they lacked ambition.

Chapon felt lucky to have it all. He would boast in the Lord, and the Lord would take care of him.

That night, there was a power outage.

Angie knocked on his door. She asked, "You got light?"

"Of course," he replied.

Then, he looked in the direction she pointed. The street lights were dark. No one had a porch light. They couldn't even see the glow coming from Canal Street.

Chapon hadn't even considered whether his electricity worked. He spent most every evening praying and fasting in the dark.

Still, he welcomed Angie and assured her. "Something ought to turn on," he said.

She tripped over his bucket of paint almost as soon as she entered the front room.

"I'm so sorry," she said when she felt the gallon can flop sideways to the floor and heard the thick paint gurgling out.

"Not to worry, cheri," Chapon addressed Angie with the words he reserved for his closest female friends. He hadn't used the word in a long, long time.

He had used it consistently with his wife when they dated. "Cheri, sit close," he said to her when they attended mass in the empty front pews, joined parishioners at the picnic tables on their outings to City Park, and partook in the dinner-dances held in the parochial school cafeteria.

"You are my only one," he said. He didn't lie. She was his first and so far, his last. They had made love, not like ducks take to water, but more like ducks running a race. She agreed to marry him when she immediately became pregnant.

"I'm a good girl, and everybody needs to know that," she said as her way of telling him that "Yes."

It seemed like every time they made love after that she was carrying a child. He later found out that the children were not necessarily his.

Still, his heart broke when she left with the seven children. Later, he turned to religion and left the empty house too.

Once, he heard his wife and children lived across town. But that could have been like another country. Chapon rarely left the neighborhood. He didn't drive anymore, only walked. He even forgot the names of the streets on the other side of town. He didn't have pockets anymore to carry bus fare.

When Angie entered his house, he saw so many possibilities.

As they tiptoed through the wet, black paint, he assured her that all was well.

"Don't worry about that," he told her, knowing that she couldn't make out what she was stepping in.

"Let's go into my sanctuary," he added, leading her into the kitchen. On the stove was a pot of coffee, dripping since the morning.

The liquid was so rich, Chapon had to dilute it with a half cup of water to make it passable.

"Sit down. It's safer than you tripping over anything else," he said as he poured the coffee, and she waited near the moonlit stove.

"I was wondering if you had electricity," Angie asked again.

"Let's see," he said and tried to turn on the kitchen light. He flipped the switch up and down several times, until Angie said, "Oh no! Stop, you're going to break something!"

Chapon heard mistrust in her voice, and he wondered how could she accept his hospitality and yet not have the respect for him that his offering of coffee deserved. He wondered if she had the devil in her.

So he put down his head and began to pray. It was a litany from the St. Jude novena, the saint of impossible causes.

"Excuse me?" Angie said. She was a single woman, but she had been around enough to know this was not normal. St. Jude was an important saint. People only prayed to St. Jude when they were very desperate. Maybe a few quick lines to St. Anthony to find the light might have been more appropriate. But a litany in the dark? Odd.

"Help us, St. Jude. Give us your aid. Bring us to the heavenly light. Give us your enlightenment."

"I really think it is time for me to go, Mr. Chapon," Angie said.

He got even louder, "Get us out of the shadows!"

"I'm going now," Angie got up from the table and started feeling her way to the front door.

That's when it happened. Behind her the kitchen light came on.

"Hallelujah," Chapon said.

The lights up and down the street came on too.

"Lord be praised. He answers prayers," Chapon shouted.

Angie kept walking toward the door. The screen door clicked behind her.

Chapon laid down in the paint in his front room floor and began doing a back stroke. He made butterfly patterns all across his living room. But nobody saw them until later.

When he got up the next day, he was mottled all over with black paint and disheveled. He had gone into such reverie that he had fallen asleep in the wet paint. His hair had bits of food stuck in it. His sheet looked like he had gone to the bathroom on himself. One foot was bare because his slipper was stuck to the living room floor. So he just wore the other.

He climbed up his ladder to write "NEAR" on his church sign, and Angie was watching. It was a message, she figured, from God.

So Angie walked to the phone and called 411 for the Mental Ward at Charity Hospital. Later, two men came in a white truck with white coats and knocked on Chapon's door, his prophecy confirmed.

Love and Its Languages

Bird Whistle

Bird Woman is at my fence again today. I know it is she because of the sound. She creeps up to the edge of my front garden near the bird feeder and whistles. She stands as motionless as a doe, hoping, I think, to blend in. As if the birds might think she is one of them. Unlikely. She is large and square, and with that flower print dress, they'd more likely believe her to be a bush than a bird. Still, she whistles to them beautifully. And, actually, some of them gather around.

In years past when Bird Woman stood at the fence, my wife went outside to greet her. She walked to the sidewalk with a warm, buttered croissant that they shared. Merrill wore her blue chenille robe, tied at the waist, and she'd take her coffee to the sidewalk and sip while Bird Woman ate and nodded.

My wife, Merrill, knew her since childhood. Even then she didn't speak.

"So what do you do at the gate?" I asked Merrill once when she returned to the kitchen after staying so long in the yard.

"We talk," she answered.

"You don't talk together," I joked.

Merrill didn't reply. Not with her voice. Instead, she looked at me with slanted, soft eyes, not hurt but disappointed. The look said that an old man like me should have known better than to laugh at others' miseries.

I slipped. I do slip sometimes. I have a cruel streak. It's not my best quality.

"We have things in common," she said.

That time, I kept my mouth shut.

It was years ago, but I still remember changing the subject, "May I join you for coffee?"

She already had the cup and was walking toward me.

That is the image I see so often when I wake up, get up, and sit by the kitchen table—her lean, graceful body in the blue robe, her permed gray curls falling away from the soft matted roots. She is carrying my coffee in one hand and hers in the other.

She smells like the flowers on our misbelief tree.

A young woman, a transplant to the neighborhood, once corrected me to say that the real name of the plant was Japanese plum. She would have continued to rant about the Latin, botanical, designation had I not stopped her and reminded her, "It is misbelief in New Orleans. Isn't that easier?"

That young woman was nothing like my Merrill, who never wasted her energy for impractical reasons.

I can imagine her now in the doorway, calling me to begin my day. It is because of her that I still rise, pull a suit out of the closet, and head to the shower.

I met my wife in college. She was studying to be a teacher and singing with the student opera club on the weekends. She was full of ego and optimism then. She prided herself on her high notes, particularly her lilting warble in *Carmen*. I have a frayed picture of her, head thrown back, then-auburn curls cascading, hands on her high hips just below her tiny waist. She is mid-Aria.

I was in pharmacy school, hoping to become pre-med in one of the first classes at Xavier. So I had no time for clubs or dates. The one time I did go out, a girl sniffed me and said I smelled like cheap liquor.

I corrected her, "Formaldehyde."

Only after a bad week of studying, tests, and stressful evenings at the library did I allow my friends to convince me to come out to one of the college performances. It was *Carmen*, of course. By the end of the evening, I was humming.

Still, I waited almost a year—watching Merrill as she walked across campus, spying at her over the tops of my sandwiches, dropping my books to stare when she passed by—before I spoke to her.

I had my letter of acceptance to medical school in my hand when I asked her out.

She read it, folded it up, and handed it back to me.

"You didn't need to wait so long," she said.

We spent one afternoon riding the bus to the lakefront, sitting on the steps and watching the waves. She brought thin chicken sandwiches on white bread with the ends removed. She had wrapped them in wax paper. After a few dates, we began holding hands.

Then, I went away. From medical school, I read the articles about her in the colored newspaper—her stage appearances, attendance at club luncheons, appointment to the elementary school—and I worked hard to return home.

I was making plans to get on at Flint-Goodrich Hospital when she wrote to me that she had received a scholarship to the Sorbonne. She was so excited, her letter was filled with exclamation points. But she knew I wouldn't be able to see her before she left town. Maybe I would meet her in Paris, she wrote and sketched a smile.

If I didn't have the money to get back to New Orleans before getting a job, I sure couldn't pay for a trip abroad.

I see when I peer through the curtains that Bird Woman has left the gate. She still comes around even though Merrill is gone. Her whistles begin sometimes when I am in my deepest morning sleep. I suspect she is trying to spot a particular kind of bird.

Once when Merrill was alive, Bird Woman came so early in the morning that I wanted to open the front door and shout at her, "Please, some people are sleeping even if you aren't!"

I had already put the pillow over my ears, raised the white noise of my radio and started reciting memorized formulas in my mind.

Merrill was already up and out of the room. I suspect that she returned to our bedroom because she heard the radio buzzing.

"Listen, can't I just go and straighten this out?" I told her in anticipation of her going outside instead and encouraging this madness.

"No, you listen," she told me, "Listen." She put her hand on my arm, knowing I'm a sucker for touch. I quieted a little.

Bird Woman's sounds were almost the perfect imitations of the birds that visited our garden, and, I expect, hers: The twang of the bob-white, the screech of the mockingbird, and the chirp of a robin—so weak that one bird alone was nearly imperceptible.

Merrill and I looked through the curtains together. The darkness of morning had just lifted but Bird Woman was still standing in shadow. The daily mist glowed around her silhouette. She had spotted a hummingbird and her head was cocked to take in the sound of the wings, manic fluttering that sprinted the bird from one flower to the next. The bird was one spot of yellow that darted in front of Bird Woman, behind her and then to the side. Bird Woman stood still, her face in awe as if she had seen an apparition.

The mist was so heavy near the ground that Bird Woman seemed to be levitating slightly above the wet grass. I rubbed the sleep out of my eyes so that I could see her ankles.

They were there.

And then our other neighbors appeared. They slammed their car doors as they left for their jobs. Then, the dogs began barking at the garbage men. Then, the chain-link gates slammed with sequential clinks as children departed for school.

Merrill never got to the Sorbonne. World War II began. Paris was off limits. And soon after, her father lost his job and she became the family breadwinner. Her opera career vanished. She stopped singing. The light in her dimmed.

My residency at Flint-Goodrich didn't give us much time to date, only a few moments to meet between her job and mine. Still, they were my sunrise.

One early morning at the empty bus-stop, I got on one knee, gave her a little fleck of a diamond, and asked her to be my wife.

Nothing could have compared to her smile.

In a few years, as a doctor's wife, she was able to keep up some of her activities—the volunteer work, women's club, and support of the college opera association. She appreciated the music but she didn't sing, except around the house.

If I was lucky enough to be home, I stopped my chores to get closer to where she stood—washing dishes in the kitchen, folding towels in the laundry room, or cleaning the bathroom—and I'd listen without comment. The one time I did try to insist that she join a choir, she told me to mind my own business.

It was one of our rare arguments. I had invaded her privacy, she said. Didn't she deserve any?

I had to grant her that much. I suspect that she thought singing was a young person's game. She was right. Her moment had passed.

With her time then, Merrill took care of the family. On Sundays, we picked up her parents and brought them to church, first in my old blue Ford and then in our beige Cadillac. Later, all of her relatives came here for dinner. Merrill collected silver trays and soup tureens, punch bowls and ladles. She bought three sets of fine china so that we could invite as many cousins and friends as possible for the holidays. Even their children used the good plates and silver, and learned to wash them and put them away.

Then, little by little, the serving ware became dusty again as everyone we knew died or moved to the new areas.

The professional people like us, then their children, went to the suburbs where they could have driveways, refrigerators, and freezers that the house-wiring could support and yards so their grandchildren could play catch without dodging an increasing number of cars in the street.

I wanted to go. But Merrill insisted we already had put down roots. She said oaks didn't transplant well, but they did grow stronger with age. What could I do? She was the oak. I stayed where I had made my nest.

She shouldn't be gone now. She was supposed to have lasted me out.

I don't have rounds at the hospital anymore. I just visit a few old patients. I can still walk to some. My universe is the few square blocks around here. I think I must share it with Bird Woman. On one corner is a grocery store and, on another, a liquor store. The third in the square holds a music school. The house that Merrill and I bought takes up the forth corner—a large lot on Broad Street. It once sat across from a wide, green neutral ground. Now the grass collects tossed-aside bottles and plastic bags.

I keep my Cadillac well-tuned just for emergencies or the odd ride to the store. There is always someone stopping to bring me food. Every few days it seems. So I don't complain.

In fact, Bird Woman provides me with too much excitement. This morning was like mating season, the racket she made.

I didn't go out to the fence like Merrill. But I usually will open the door and wave. That seems to calm her down. She will make her loudest racket if she hasn't seen me in a few days. I didn't have the strength for her this morning though. After a while, she left.

Later, on my way out to the car, I refill the bird feeder with sugar water, and I throw the ends of the toast out for the sparrows. There is a brown flock in no time. They're not afraid to gather near me and are practically in my way as I open the car door.

When Merrill was alive, I always opened the door for her. She sat on the side nearest to the curb. I made sure to park the car in that manner at night. That way I could open her door, and then walk around to open mine on the street.

Every time, she said, watch out for the cars, as if I were a child and unable to cross the traffic. This morning there is a car coming when I go to the driver's side. So I wait.

But the car stops. There are men I don't know. They ask my name.

"Dr. Bolden from Charity," I respond. "And you are?"

Isaac, Pete, Aaron, they tell me. They hesitate before giving me their names, so I wonder if they are telling the truth.

"You live here?" one asks.

I nod yes. That seems to satisfy them enough to keep going.

The neighborhood is different now. People have become suspicious of one another. People like us, once poor and then professional, who had worked our ways up—in segregation by making our own self-help clubs, leaving the United States for schooling, and then breaking the barriers with legislation and marching—are oddities to young men who don't own suit coats or leather shoes. Young women point me out to their children sometimes when I sit on the porch as if I am part of a field trip. Other people, nervous and thin, try to come through the gate when

I'm sitting to ask me for money or food. I offer them yard-work—
which they refuse—then tell them to leave, and they curse me. My
first instinct is to return the greeting. But my better judgment says
that could be dangerous.

Merrill was a patient woman. We were not only going to
stay where we lived, she insisted, we were going to provide shade to
the neighborhood. She gardened fearlessly in the front yard despite
the bullet holes that appeared on our house and the ones nearby. She
grew exotic plants and flowers to bring the birds. She decorated the
porch with blossoms and even big, potted trees until someone came
up to the house in the middle of the night with a truck and carted
them off.

"They weren't our local thieves," she joked, "those were
professionals. Probably from the suburbs."

She continued to hand around seedlings to our neighbors
until our block was full of blooms that began in our garden.

All of our neighbors showed up at her wake and funeral.
They filled my refrigerator with food. There were big casseroles that
took a week to eat, even after I shared them with visitors. There
were desserts that were so sweet, the tears came to my eyes. In the
back of the freezer were the small dishes Merrill herself had made
just for me.

Just before I semi-retired, Merrill began to go on house calls
with me. She cooked our meals before we left the house and froze
them so that when we returned we would have food.

One night, she helped me as I went to deliver a baby. It
must have been two decades earlier. The woman around the corner
was in labor. Someone came to knock on our door. Merrill and I
took a flashlight and negotiated our way in the dark. "The blind
leading the blind," she joked on the way back. The streetlights were
out because some of the young people had taken to shooting b-b
guns at the streetlights and tossing their sneakers on them. I couldn't
figure out the attraction.

The woman in labor did not have time to go to the hospital, and the teenager who brought us to the house seemed to be in charge. I went to the bedroom while Merrill stayed in the front room with the teenager and the other children. Every time, their mother strained, I could hear them cry.

Then I heard the front door slam, Merrill had taken them outside to the dark front porch.

The baby came quickly after that. I was able to swaddle it with a towel and call an ambulance. It was a boy.

I went to tell Merrill and the children outside. She had closed the windows and doors so the children would not hear the labor. When I opened the screen, I heard her singing and them following softly along.

I don't know why I remember this as I get into my car to see a few old patients.

The young men are sitting on the step of the abandoned house next door when I come home just before dark. I wave and go inside.

The last of Merrill's prepared dishes is still in the freezer. Her cooked meals once stacked the shelves so that I also could have a warm dish if I ever came home and she was asleep. I don't think there will ever be a good time to warm this last one.

I fix myself scrambled eggs and toast for dinner. I watch television. I read a book. I make a few phone calls then go to bed.

I dream of Bird Woman. She is a cardinal that lands in the green grass. It picks at seeds for a while and then flies off. I hope death comes to me like that.

I toss and turn in bed. Merrill is not here.

I finally get to sleep, then there is banging on the door.

I open it. Pete and Aaron are holding the third one.

"Hey," Pete says. They push inside

The shirt of the third is soaked with blood.

"You should bring this man to a hospital," I say.

"Not happening," Aaron responds.

"Do something," says Pete.

I can see it's a gunshot wound, and I have been designated to fix it. I don't say anything. I cannot extrude the bullet and, without letting him know that, I get my bag to patch him. I have a little topical anesthesia, but luckily no opiates that might inspire them to worse crimes. I give the victim a few shots of good whiskey and while his friends drink the rest, I stitch the skin closed. I offer him antibiotics and try to send them away.

Instead, they begin to fall asleep on my sofa.

Against my will, but exhausted, so do I.

It is still dark when they wake me up.

"Doc, give us something to eat on the road," Pete says.

He is in my refrigerator taking bread and meat to make sandwiches. He takes sodas and beer. He moves to the freezer to see what it contains. His hand lights on Merrill's last meal.

I tense and he can see it.

"What's this?"

"You don't want it," I answer.

In reality, it is probably only just a little turkey from an ancient Thanksgiving party with gravy, cornbread stuffing, and peas. I think of giving him the menu, but I hear myself saying, "Don't touch it. It's mine."

He takes the food out of the freezer, and he waves the container in front of my nose.

I say quietly, "Please leave it alone." I am fairly growling. But he has no subtlety. To him, it's a good time to play the fool.

He is waving the food away from me in figure eights then pushes it into the microwave. As he turns from me and presses the button, I rush to reach the plastic container. He blocks the way.

I push him and he trips backwards, and I fall in his direction. He curses at me as I hit the ground. He prepares to give me a kick. But his crony hurries in to stop him. For this, he gets cursed as well. As they hurl expletives at one another, I steady myself and get up. They are both glaring at me once they settle down. I am glaring back in a stand-off.

I continue to breathe hard. I can feel that my pajama bottoms have slipped past my waist. I pull them up and stand evenly on two feet. The microwave beeps, and the crook puts the food on the table.

Then we all hear it. There is whistling along the fence line. At first, it is barely audible. Then it gets louder and louder.

"What the hell?" says Pete.

Merrill and Bird Woman had a standing code that if they didn't see one another in a week that one of them would check on the other. I don't know how they arranged this. But my wife told me that they had an agreement.

In her stead, I had been waving regularly to Bird Woman. But this week, I've been hiding from her.

She is whistling louder and louder. Now, I hear her footsteps on the porch. There is a knock and whistling at the door.

"Damn. She is going to wake up the neighborhood," Pete says, "Shut her up."

"She's coming for food," I tell the men, and I quickly grab the plastic container and head for the door.

At the porch, I hand it to Bird Woman. "Merrill wanted you to have this," I say.

She takes it, having no sense of time, and, probably a fluid conception of death.

I hear the back door slam. The men have run away. I rush into the house to secure the back lock.

Then, I return to the front again to find Bird Woman. She hasn't gotten far. She has opened the plastic container, picked out hot bits of the meal, and is cooling them in her open hands. Then, she is scattering food to the sparrows. Some catch it in mid-air.

What Went Missing

Driving without a License

"I was hurrying to get the cat's eye drops," I give the reason for my speeding to the officer. He is a cool drink of water—young and healthy, dimples in his cheeks. He is looking kindly at me and seems to be somewhat amused as if I were his mother. "The cat, Winky, is going blind in both eyes and keeps running into the furniture."

He wants to laugh, so I say it more seriously, squinting so the water rises to my pupils. "If he hits one more thing, he might get a brain hemorrhage." I draw out the last word with all its syllables. "Hem-more-edge." Like devastated and incapacitated, it's a good word.

He asks me for my license, but I know that's just routine. It's required, but some cops make an exception. I appear contrite so that he will bend the rules.

"I never, never should have gotten behind the wheel in this state." It slips out quickly, but I hope he'll interpret it.

People say the police in North Carolina are the worst. Maybe even worse than Louisiana. Thankfully, the cop believes that I am shaken up. He leans in toward the window.

I panic momentarily. I cannot let him see what's on the floor. He might see Gary, my semi-automatic pistol. Gary goes with me everywhere. When people telephone, and there are hardly any these days, except my daughter and the telemarketers, I tell them, "Let me first consult with Gary in the living room." And people think I've got the protection of a man.

I'll have to figure out an excuse for my daughter when I see her. "Gary's back at home." Or "Gary went to his artillery reunion."

Something that will discourage her from asking questions. She's had enough confusion since her father left. Then I left, and she went to stay with strangers.

Most of her life, she has shown about as much interest in me as I did in her. Fair enough.

I didn't call when she entered grade school or even when she graduated college. Why bother her with a litany of bad choices—the jobs I quit, the places I slept. Entertain her with stories of small hotels along mundane two-lane highways, the smells of moldy icemakers in the hall?

Should I tell her that I followed one pill then another, then my own mind—all of them sending me, careening, to dark corners? What else was left for me but to quietly disappear?

At least, I didn't make another child. I didn't do that. And who would love me now if they saw me? A body like a winter tree, a face that needed watering? When I was younger, the men that I took to bed were like this boy here, this silly, pretty officer. Too young to know they weren't smart enough. Too self-absorbed to realize that they soon would become collateral damage. I was a raging flood, going everywhere, bulldozing everything, and following my jagged bedrock.

When my daughter called last night and said that she'd finally like to see me, I took off to see her.

I thought, "Thank you, God." Finally, the one person who might look at me with pity.

"The cat's alone now," I plead with the officer. He does not ask to see my license, just tells me that I must slow down, and he waves my car away.

I don't have a cat or a dog. I'm not even carrying a suit-case. Everything is new from now on.

I am driving a car that I got from a former friend. It was in the middle of the night. He was sleeping in a house that I had visited once or twice before. I knew that his keys hung on the wall, a hook in the living room. But I knew that he would not allow me to sleep over. So, I hitched a ride to the road near his house. I went into the woods. I found a stump that wasn't damp and sat.

The grey sky faded into darkness. The birds piped down. The locusts crackled all around me. I didn't move until I heard the rustling brush. Then, I stomped my feet every few minutes. I'm not a fan of snakes.

The car was unlocked, of course. No one locks his car when his house is so far off the highway. I hotwired the ignition and took off. I thought I saw the lights come on from his bedroom when I pulled away. But he wasn't going to report the stolen car to the police because they'd have a lot of questions for him first.

My daughter asked me why I left so long ago, and I couldn't tell her the answer. The memories are too strong. Her face was round and unmarked, pale and angelic. Her hair was thin and curled around her forehead. Her eyes were narrow. One relative asked if her father was Chinese. That was one of the first clues that I had to get going. I couldn't watch the shade come down over her face as I knew it would if I stayed. And I wasn't the type to settle in dull, little New Orleans.

In no time, my name would have made the rounds of gossip because I couldn't spend every night sitting on the porch or in the kitchen. They would see me at the gas station, at the racetrack or at the bar, and the rumors would begin again.

But I am moving fast now, since my daughter called to see me. I'm hitting 60, 70, 80, 90 miles per hour. I need to go faster or not to go there at all. My girl was as tall as the table top when I saw her last. She could peer across the table's surface and see there was no food. She needed more to eat, a place to sleep, and better clothes than I could provide alone. I left her on a step, and I took off.

Since she's grown and I got older, I began to wonder. Maybe I should have become the kind of woman who stood at the stove every evening, stirring something cheap but nourishing, or someone who sewed skirts, and knitted sweaters, and shopped daily at the farm stands. Maybe I could have led her to her school and walked inside the classroom, smoothing her pretty red hair as I left. I could have had a house smelling of oak fireplaces, dinner, and cleanliness that people show as love.

I can now imagine places like this. Over the years, I saw them when I delivered groceries, washed the elderly sick in their homes, and came to polish floors.

While my employers took vigils watching me for theft from their kitchen counters and open doorways, I pretended that I belonged in places like this.

But I was a paper doll taped over their perfect picture books, a stranger in their bathroom mirrors, the lame dog that stayed around their steps long after they stopped throwing scraps into the yard.

Maybe now, I'm ready to come inside.

My daughter tells me that she lives in a "suburban village." It's a place where people become neighbors on purpose. They have thought long and hard about having friends who work every day, whose children have so much that they volunteer to give things away, and who make rules to permit only certain kinds of behaviors in public. There is a local train that pulls into her stop—but only weekdays—a few stores on a paved strip with a brick sidewalk, and a clean courtyard where she "snacks" outside. Inside their homes, they pull drinks from wooden cabinets and sometimes smoke a bit of hash, importing bags from houses behind truck stops, the kinds of places I was likely to be found. Now, I am trafficking myself to respectability.

The pine trees rush past. The highway flies up in front of me like a ribbon. The dotted lines make ghosts on my eyeballs. The highway separates into where I've come from and where I'm going. I'm rushing forward.

I hear the faint sound of a cop car's siren. I can't let that slow me down. I am almost to my daughter's exit. Like a gas station billboard, the sign in my head says, "Forgiveness Last Chance."

I drive faster. I hold the steering wheel tightly as it shudders. My palms are sweating. I floor the accelerator. The car jerks forward. Everything on either side of me is blurry. The cop car gets louder, gaining on me. I pump the gas. I have to get there today. I do not want my daughter to think about me too much. She might change her mind.

I will finally have someone to lift my burdens. I'll accept her guilt, obligation, or compassion.

"Love is messy," I will tell her as my explanation.

I hit the accelerator harder. I stomp it like I'm killing bugs.

Suddenly there is a bang. The car will not go faster. It slows down to a halt.

The cop gets out of his vehicle. He's coming up beside the car.

I see in my side mirror that it is the same beautiful boy. He is so healthy—strong jaws, good complexion, posture of an athlete. He's even pretty when he is not smiling. His mother must have taken good care of him. He walks with confidence as if someone hugs him in the morning every day before he leaves the house. Someone has looked at him with admiration all of his life.

Some people are just lucky. Others have to make their luck.

Gary could solve my problem easily. I could reach down to my floor mat, pick up Gary, and blow this boy away. I could commandeer his car. I could dump his vehicle someplace then steal another. We're on an empty highway. No one would ever know.

His mother would be looking for him. Then, she could join the club of loved and lost. And I could show up at my daughter's door—on time, just twenty or so years behind her life, but finally there, nonetheless.

I can imagine the look in her eyes now—excitement, and elation—to see her mother. But a scrawny, hungry, hangdog. I also see her disappointment.

I saw that look so often when she was a little girl. The worry when she walked with me into a room. The eyes turned down, her face becoming long and thin. It started to resemble mine.

"I'm going to see my daughter," I tell the cop now at my car door. "She wants to meet me. I haven't seen her since she was a toddler." I wonder if he's going to believe this one.

"You're not going to see her if you speed like that," he says. He understands more than he knows.

If I had just gone faster, my car could have taken control. It could have spun out, tumbled off the road, sent my body flying as it should have many years ago. I put both wrists out the window to get cuffed. "Take me, officer," I say it with a smile.

The cop leans forward and sees Gary winking from the floor. I see a look of horror show unintentionally across his face. He slaps on the cuffs with gusto and gets his telephone for backup.

At her comfortable home, my daughter waits. I've seen the photos. It's a pretty house. She has an upstairs and a downstairs. She has bathrooms, a kitchen, a dining and a living room. She has a pool where she sits with people who don't raise their voices.

They'll be talking about me tonight. She'll be telling everyone that I was always lazy, unruly, and uncaring. Why should she have expected that I would change now?

She'll never see me. Hopefully, she'll never want to see me again. That's how much I love her.

Maurice in New York City

When Maurice returned to New York City, he hated it because nobody said hello. Worse than that, people would look at him and stare momentarily before going on to the next person in the subway. Stare at him and never nod to acknowledge his presence, as if they were looking at a piece of furniture they had no desire to buy.

He wanted, at those times, to jump in their faces and shout, "Hey, say hello. What's wrong with you?" But that would have been a bad move. He knew, even though he was not from New York City, because he was from a city himself, New Orleans where that kind of behavior was likely to get him shot.

So he rode the subways as anonymously as everyone else did. Not looking at anyone in the eye. Not smiling at a girl, even though her face was a few inches from his. Maurice got on the train, rode to the addresses on his piece of paper, delivered the courier company's packages, and went home to the fourth floor walkup at the edge of the Bronx. By the end of the day, he was exhausted from the sheer pain of being ignored.

No one called him. No one visited. He told no one where he was. As far as they knew, he had drowned running away from the police. Gone. Swoosh. Disappeared like foam in an undertow. He had called Myra that morning before he went fishing.

"All right, babe. I'm bringing you a big redfish tonight. Going to make me a courtboullion?"

"Croakers and catfish, that's what I'm thinking."

"You'll see. Preheat the oven."

"The oven is always hot."

He laughed.

That girl knew him well, and also how to give a man a good send off so that he wanted to get back home.

He had planned to return to her house by three in the afternoon, a long 12-hour day—driving to fish, fishing, and coming home. He had planned it perfectly.

He left work before the sky had any pink. He knew that time of day well. Just before dawn, the tourists were leaving the French Quarter bars and the previous night's shift of prostitutes and crossdressers were finally sitting down. Their makeup gave their cheeks an unnatural florescence. Their wigs sat on the bar and sometimes slipped off to the floor.

"Oh, Lord, a rat!" One night, a patron stepped on a furry, damp thing in the dark along the bottom of the counter where Maurice had tended bar. He got a broom and beat the shadowy thing until a man exclaimed he had murdered someone's hairpiece.

"Killer" became his nickname after that. A joke because of the quickly circulated story that climaxed with his stabbing the hair with the broom. ("I should have got it on my cell phone," the regulars nodded to one another.)

They also found the name hilarious because for all his stocky strength, Maurice hardly raised his voice. At 4 a.m., he sometimes had whispered conversations with the clients late at night, mostly about love. The men, usually, who still sat at the counter were always alone.

"I tried to settle down but do you know how difficult that is," said a young man one night with a round face and curly black hair. He tastefully wore lipstick and eye-makeup. "It's hard to find a companion."

Maurice replied, "Yes. I'm still waiting for my one and only."

"I hope you find someone gorgeous."

"Simple will be just fine."

They toasted with full shot glasses of scotch.

Also in the early morning hours, Maurice's father had once confessed to him, "You can love more than one woman, you know." He had seated himself alongside Maurice's childhood bed. As his father spoke and Maurice slowly woke up, he still couldn't quite understand. Maurice couldn't imagine his father with anyone beside his mother. But as he got older, Maurice began to understand that love was very complicated.

Who among his friends and relatives had complete trust? His friend Melvin spent weeks complaining about his girlfriend Reina, then married her when she got pregnant. Joe LaRose, who had owned the bar where Maurice worked, was seeing a sister on the side while his white wife, and in the eyes of his family his perfect match, buzzed around her Metairie House hanging Christmas decorations.

He was getting off work and standing at the bus stop on Esplanade and Claiborne when he met Myra. She was on her way to Charity Hospital. Her shift began at 4:30 a.m. She asked to stand next to him for protection.

"You know how many times people stop, ask me if I want a ride? From a stranger?" she looked at him incredulously as if she had known him all her life.

"They come up, ask, 'Baby, I take you anywhere you want to go.' Criminal punks. Half of them ain't got hair under their arms.

Get out the car, they come up to here." She raised her hand to chest level to show Maurice the height and laughed.

He smiled. She sure could tell a story.

"I seen you," she told him then. "I'm not crazy. I seen you many times. You good."

He tipped an imaginary hat and bowed, nervous and overformal. She was fine. Stacked, even in her orderly uniform. He was a sucker for ironed clothes because of his Catholic school training. The excessive neatness suggested to him that she also had a clean house, clean kitchen, and clean body. He moved close enough to smell her.

She noticed but did not back away.

They met like that for many early mornings. She came bringing a story as payment for his protection—about the evening she lost her shoes in a nightclub, the Saturday she went to church thinking it was Sunday, the time she burned the turkey necks on the grill watching the Saints play. She always made him laugh before the bus arrived. The air brakes squeaked, the doors opened with a whoosh and Maurice gestured for her to go up the steps first. At first he did it as if he were her carriage driver—a big sweep of his hand, and she entered like Queen Elizabeth. Then, after they became more familiar, he nodded in her direction, and she knew what he meant.

They sat separately for the ride. She sat in one of the front seats. He sat in the back.

Literally a month of Sundays passed, then Mardi Gras, and he told her that he wasn't going to be waiting with her anymore because he was laid off.

"Why don't you come to see me?" she said.

He took the invitation. Then, they dated. He came to her house at about 9 p.m., the time he usually would have gone to work at the bar. For a while, they sat on the sofa, rumpling the cotton slipcover as they inched closer to one another. They watched television and admired Myra's collection of travel souvenirs. On a crocheted doily were a heavy glass mug from Lafayette, miniatures of the Washington monument and the Houston Astrodome, and a pink ceramic Las Vegas dancer—all mementos of other peoples' vacations.

After Maurice and Myra had sex, they slept for a few hours before he brought her to work. She never told him about whether she had a man, and he didn't ask. He didn't want her to question him about his past. He had been dating since about the third grade and none of his girlfriends or their families had forgotten. He remembered them too in the way people in small towns can list one another's relatives, previous addresses (the houses not the numbers), and classmates. Everyone also knew that he had not loved their daughters. And they also knew the reason that love made him skittish. His family did not keep their business behind closed doors.

The aroma of burnt dust rose as the steam hissed in the New York radiator pipes. Then they clanked. Maurice would never get accustomed to this noise. It reminded him of his days as a mechanic. He really didn't know the job. Half the time he just banged against the engine with a long-armed wrench. But the drivers knew less. Maurice quoted them huge amounts to fix their cars. Then, he called one of his cousins to do him the favors. Every time he fixed a car, he could ride around in it for three days. Who knew what he did on his joy-rides? It was a fair trade. The car got fixed. The driver paid. And Maurice made enough money to get over for a few more weeks.

He was on his last deposit from one of those paychecks and nothing else was going to come from anywhere else. But rather than worry about his situation, that morning he decided to go fishing.

At the lake in the dark, he lowered the borrowed skiff down the bank. He felt the stern swaying as he eased it into the water. He felt his way into the boat, loaded in his gear, ripped the manual ignition, and took off. The sun began to rise. He could just make out the outlines of trees on shore. He was out far enough. He dropped a line, and his mind filled the silence with Myra's confession just before he had hung up the phone.

"My boyfriend's back in town."

Maurice didn't say anything, but his silence demonstrated his concern.

"That doesn't mean anything though. I'm done with him. I just thought you'd like to know."

"What does he look like?"

"He's not my type."

Maurice held his face and his body still.

"You my type."

"That's what I used to think. Where he's coming back from?"

"Angola."

"Wonderful." All Maurice needed was to meet up with an ex-con. "Are you going to see him?"

"He called but I never answered the phone. I'm done with him. I'm just with you now."

"That's what I used to think."

"Really, baby. Really."

That's when a reasonable person would have dropped her. He heard the lie in her words. If she hadn't picked up the phone, how would she know that the man had returned? But maybe she just heard a rumor. Maurice had wanted to ask her. Maybe he should have.

He and Myra had become close on their later bus rides. Just before he had lost his job, they began to sit together. She confided to him that she had always wanted to have children and to finish high school. She said that her boss tried to feel her up, and she didn't know how to respond. She told him that she hated the laundromat because that's where her mother worked until one hot summer day when she died there of a heart attack. Myra told him about her life so easily, Maurice began to like her. It was better than love.

He knew love from a couple of hard times. Love had all the symptoms of a low-grade flu that altered into something life-threatening. He felt passionate for a girl at 16, then followed her around school, watching her every movement, until she reported him. Many years later, he loved a woman, and he thought the feeling was mutual. Then, she moved to another city. That time, he felt achy and breathless for months. He called her on the phone often, but couldn't continue the conversations because he had to lay down. He couldn't understand the way she spoke calmly to him while his stomach lurched, his body trembled, and the blood roared in his ears. He needed to hold her. Finally, he simply medicated his attraction to women with alcohol, so they rarely involved themselves with him.

But he had no problem sleeping with a friend like Myra. She touched him in all his favorite spots. He had told her about them while they were commuting—the things that got him started, the things that made him smile and open his eyes wide, and what made him go "Oh, la-la." Myra appreciated his humor. And she even laughed when they were in bed together, and he did too, because they were having so much fun.

So when she told him she would not see the ex-con, even though it seemed like a lie, he wanted to believe it.

But she had called the ex-con her boyfriend, and that nagged Maurice. Still, he wasn't going to mess up good sex or their sleep or the meals she had waiting for him to arrive. It was all too perfect. He concentrated on fishing.

He sat in the skiff on the smooth water. There were just him, the mosquito hawks, and the mosquitos—all wondering who was going to benefit most from the day. Maurice did make a catch, and as he predicted, it was a red fish. That gave him more faith. Proof that he and Myra were meant to be together.

He called his friend on the cell phone on the way back to her house.

"An ex-con? And she's just now telling you?" his friend asked.

"What? You think I should be bothered?" he replied.

"I wouldn't surprise her at any time, unless I'm bringing a piece."

"You know I don't carry no piece," Maurice answered. "If you see anything in the paper tomorrow, though, don't come looking for me," he laughed.

"Man, don't be too crazy for your own good."

The one thing about New York that Maurice could never get over was the number of people. He could get lost in the crowd. Every once in a while, he thought he recognized a face. But he was always wrong. If there were any people from New Orleans, they had forgotten the way to identify the old family resemblances so long ago that everyone was a stranger. And they had forgotten the old family manners too. No one nodded hello or invited him home.

Not that he knew anyone in New York to invite him. He had left town so suddenly. So he had no recommendations of places to eat, people to call, things to see. He just went now from his apartment in the Bronx to his job delivering packages. He could figure out the locations from the addresses. Most streets were numbered, not named, like in New Orleans, for dreams, saints, and myths.

Down South, a person couldn't go to the doors delivering packages without the dogs, neighbors, and friends needing attention. The dogs needed to be petted or tied up. The neighbors had to know what you were doing. The friends who saw you driving a truck wanted a ride, or a jump start, or for you to pick up a few items on your way back.

He could have never delivered packages the way he did now. People just signed their names where he told them. Sometimes they gave him a tip. Every time, they had him stand outside the door in the long, empty hallway and then, after they got what they wanted, they closed the door, leaving him alone without a word of goodbye. And every hallway looked the same. At one end was an ugly red sign that said "Exit." But it was never the one he wanted. Sometimes, he felt that he should rush into the recipient's apartment—since he wasn't going to get an invitation—to see how they lived, where they sat, what they ate. Other times, he felt that he could rush right into the kitchen, grab a knife out of the kitchen drawer, and slit his own throat.

Usually, a few shots of vodka from his pocket flask kept that feeling away.

He did like one thing about New York though, and that was the view from his window. He faced a bay where ducks and swans floated leisurely in the warm months, and hunkered down in cold weather. It reminded him of Lake Borgne, and the phrase "sitting ducks" came to him. He could have picked them off, if he had his shotgun, just as he had hunted and brought food to Myra's table. He did it regularly before that night.

When he had entered her house with the redfish, Myra's boyfriend was sitting at the dinner table.

"What's cooking?" Maurice asked. He spoke in an exaggeration of friendliness because he was so nervous.

"We just here," Myra answered.

"That I can see."

The boyfriend put out his hand, and Maurice hesitated for a moment. He looked at Myra and then looked at his own hand for a second. But he remembered his manners and stuck his hand out. "Maurice," he said. "You a friend of Myra, huh?" He stated the obvious and was mad at himself.

"Yea. She my friend."

"I see," Maurice answered. He went to the kitchen to put the fish into the sink and that's when he saw it—a new snow-globe on the counter. Inside of its stale water was the Empire State building and artificial flakes, without doubt a gift from the criminal. And only a few feet away was the black skillet. Maurice could swing it right at this man's head, and he could take out Myra too. He could return from the kitchen swinging like the cowboys in the movies when they stepped through the barroom doors guns blazing. They both would be sorry they tricked him.

Then he heard the door click. Maybe the ex-con was getting backup. Maybe he had come to hurt Myra and Maurice should be defending her rather than taking her out.

Before he could step toward the kitchen, Myra came to meet him.

"He gone."

Maurice didn't say anything,

Then he noticed through the glass oven door that the racks were empty of pots and pans where Myra usually kept them, and only one shiny roaster waited.

"I done already cut up the seasonings," Myra said.

He looked at her—still stacked and with an old face. She looked like a reformed drinker and smoker, although she wasn't reformed. She still went to the bars, danced with her hips wide out to the side so the men could admire her. She still called people "Boo" in the grocery stores—men and women which at first made him wonder if she was gay. Then he realized that she was just lighthearted.

And maybe even a little feeble-minded. His heart opened.

He took her in his arms, pulled her close to him, so that she could feel the manhood and said, "Let's go to New York."

He could see that she was stunned.

But she took only a minute to retort, "And leave all this here?"

He began to laugh, then stopped and wondered whether she was serious. Then he saw her laughing, and he held her closer.

The fish in the sink stank. The oven never got preheated. They went into the bedroom, and after they made love, she began to pack. She put a few pair of nylon underwear, her clean jeans, some t-shirts, a good dress, and her sparkly hoodie into her cotton grocery bag with the zipper.

Maurice filled his backpack and met her at the bus station. They had enough for the tickets and a few days at a hotel. They sat in the front near the driver and cuddled. Then Myra talked to him most of the ride while Maurice slept. They were both wide awake at midnight when the bus pulled into the midtown station. They had arrived.

They followed the bright lights and walked to the Empire State Building. This was the real thing.

They didn't need a hotel because that night, after putting their bags in a locker, they walked until dawn. They watched the lights in the skyscrapers dim at sunrise. Their twinkles disappeared like dew off the morning grass. Then the streets filled with cars and the sidewalks with people so fast that Maurice almost lost Myra a couple times. So they held hands like children.

They found a small hotel off Times Square in the day and slept until evening. The bed sheets were stiff and fresh, even if they were a little mottled. Neither Maurice nor Myra noticed. The bed felt right.

They spent another night walking and this time also emptying their pockets of change as people came to speak to them about sleeping on the streets, losing their jobs, being thrown out of their homes—sometimes by family.

"How people could get rid of their kin . . ." Myra stated when she saw a man, woman, and their two daughters huddled on the ground against a building. And Maurice finished her sentence, ". . . I don't know."

But he did and so did she.

His father wasn't home so many nights. His mother cried and moved furniture. She rearranged the front room, her bedroom, and the living room so that when he came home he tripped in the dark and fell on the hardwood. One night, she sat in the rocker with a shotgun on her lap. Maurice stayed awake to warn his father, but thankfully he didn't have to. She put the gun away before his father stumbled home in the pre-dawn.

Myra's left eyebrow was severed into two pieces by the beer bottles thrown outside her childhood house, one parent at another. The back of her right hand mostly caught the shards and was webbed with keloids. Still, she told Maurice that she had cried daily for months when both of her parents died a week apart of unrelated causes.

"I should have been there," Maurice said even though they hadn't yet met.

"What could you do?" she replied.

Maurice didn't have the word for it. He just took her in his arms, held and rocked her like a baby. She smelled of Jack and fell asleep almost immediately. Maurice felt a pang of loneliness when she began to snore lightly, even though his goal of getting her to relax had been accomplished.

The morning after her confession, although he had felt very close to her, she didn't remember anything. He watched her pencil in the eyebrow with a mismatched brown, rub a baboon ass pink color on her sallow cheeks, and lacquer on a coat of purple lipstick. Then, he kissed her goodbye before she left the house, knowing that few other people would want her. He felt safe, if not completely satisfied. No one got everything.

"You so easy to please," Myra told him on their last day in New York. He had packed their bags for the bus and made up the hotel bed. She was taking a last look out of the high-rise window.

Maurice held her on the bus home the way he held his childhood pillow, two arms wrapped around her so that his hands almost touched his forearms. He nestled her into his body, but she kept getting caught on the armrest so he gave up after a while. He slept. Then she slept as they went south down the coast and across the mountains. Half asleep, he could still hear Myra exclaim when the bus made each sharp turn. The bus angled against the road, and they were laid to the side against the window for too many seconds before they straightened up. Myra laughed like a child coming down a slide. It seemed to egg on the driver who made the turns even steeper.

For a while, Maurice sat rigid in the seat, trying to resist the sideways momentum. But he couldn't and started to feel carsick.

When Myra returned to her house, she pulled out the paper-framed picture of them in Times-Square from her suitcase. Gaudy red and blue stars surrounded them standing close together against a painted background of the skyline. She leaned the picture on her mantle against the bricked-up white-painted fireplace in the second room of her shotgun house. They could see it from her bed.

Myra got on the phone and told everyone about the heights of the buildings, the strange food they ate, and all the forms of transportation—the careening subways, the overcrowded bus and the taxi cabs that drove so fast she had thought she was going to lose her mind.

In answer to one question, she said, "Yes, with him."

She must have seen the cloud pass over Maurice's face because she looked up from her phone and winked in his direction, her florid cheek momentarily meeting her crooked brow.

She began to call him, "Sugar Daddy."

Maurice wasn't sure he liked that. But he said nothing.

Then, he got a new job.

He bought her a stove, bedspreads, and a nicer television. She put their picture in a better frame, and they went to the store and got more photos done. Big ones that looked as if they were married. She wore a white dress, and he wore a hat with a band that matched his vest. He put one small picture in his wallet.

He brought her to work in the early morning hours. In the evenings, she took a bubble bath and cooked. Then Maurice got in the car and drove to Chalmette. He was security so he watched the chain-link fences around a chemical plant because people came to steal the fittings, workers uniforms, anything that wasn't locked away. Who knew what people wanted when they had nothing?

One day he came home early and he drove up to her house. The moon was bright and the street was empty. He saw Myra sitting on the porch with the ex-con, ex-boyfriend. She was in her nightgown and slippers.

"Well, hey nah," Maurice spoke with a little more confidence this time. He had won Myra fair and square.

"I'm just going," the man said. "All right, Myra."

Maurice couldn't remember what happened next. Someone said their words had led to blows. Somebody called the cops. They sent him home.

Maurice went back to his house. It was empty and smelled of old shoes and wet towels. Nothing was still edible in the refrigerator. He had spent too much time over at Myra's house. Or maybe not enough. He couldn't figure out which.

How often had the man come over? Were they still talking? What was he to Myra? Maurice may have asked these questions. But he didn't remember the answers. All he knew was that she yelled "Stop. Stop. Stop." She yelled loud enough for the neighbors to come over.

He had plenty of time to think about his actions, and his words as he walked around the perimeter of the chemical plant most of the night, skittish as a Doberman.

That morning after work, he had a few drinks and felt better. He drove to Myra's house to ask her whether she remembered what he did. She came to the screen door in the same nightgown, slippers and a baffled look on her sallow face. He reached for the door handle, and opened it, and entered the front room. He closed the wooden door behind him and reached for her hand.

It was cold and sweating.

Her touch made Maurice remember the first time he came to her house. Then, he still believed that spending the night with someone might make him sick. He thought that, at most, they could go out a couple of times. They could drink and maybe sleep together. That would have been enough.

Instead though, she invited him in by reaching for his hand. It was clammy. She noticed, he could tell, because she flinched slightly. Still, she brought him to sit next to her on the sofa. Then she took his hands—one at a time—and rubbed them between hers to make them warm. She talked to him the whole time too as if they knew one another well. She had given him strength.

So now he took both of her hands and looked into her eyes. Her body stayed rigid. So he moved his hands up from her wrists and massaged her arms, shoulders and neck until she fell slack.

Wordlessly, he went home to get his suitcase.

On the way to his house, Maurice saw the ex-con on the street and walked over to him. Maurice pulled the picture of him and Myra from his wallet. He flipped it around for the ex-con to see. He studied it for a long time. A shadow moved over his face. The ex-con slowly reached into his inside jacket pocket. He brought out a knife. He stabbed Maurice's hand, snatched the picture, then, ran away.

Maurice shouted at him, but the man never turned around. So Maurice shut off the blood with his other hand, then wrapped his wound with a tight handkerchief. He stopped at the clinic on the way home where he told everyone the story of the stabbing. The doctor sympathized, then patched him up. Maurice went home and packed enough for a month at Myra's house.

When he arrived, a neighbor was just closing her door.

"What you doing here?" he asked Maurice. "Returning to the scene of the crime?"

Maurice stared.

"They looking for you. What happened to your hand?"

"A knife slice me," Maurice answered.

"Well, she dead. You coming to check?" The neighbor spoke to Maurice with such a flat hard voice. "Somebody call the police!" he shouted aloud.

"What are you talking about," Maurice asked.

"You kill her. I know you did," he said, "I call the police that night you all was fighting. You was going to kill her. You knowed all along."

"Oh my God," Maurice shouted. "Myra. My baby."

"Yea, now you sorry. They is all sorry."

With tears streaming, Maurice picked up his suitcase and left quickly.

"They going to get you," the neighbor called after him. "Stop him!"

But no one wanted to get involved. They just looked at one another.

Maurice went quickly to the bank and took out the money he had earned from his security job. He got on the bus and went to New York.

He eventually found an apartment in the Bronx.

There were moments, sometimes before dawn, when he walked the streets of New York and the warm breeze held his body. He knew then that the moisture from a storm in the South had finally arrived. It carried the salt from the ocean, maybe from the lake in New Orleans, and it made him want to cry.

He tried not to think about his friends, the French Quarter bars, and the summer nights that he had ridden the bus with Myra. But he couldn't help think about love—whether some people were not made for love and whether he was one of them. "Walk away, Brother," his friend Melvin had told him that night after his first fight with Myra when the cops were called. "Walk and don't look back."

Maurice was trying to do that now.

Most days, he went inside his apartment and waited for his feelings to dim as the television spouted mindless silly messages. But sometimes he couldn't help himself, and he got on the internet. He looked at the pictures of New Orleans' small houses and battered streets. Once in a while he saw a familiar person caught in a candid pose by an anonymous camera. One night, he read in the online newspaper that Myra's ex-con went back to jail for a different crime. Another time, Maurice read that he himself was wanted in the case of Myra's death.

That time, Maurice felt as if he had swallowed a block of ice. His whole body shivered and his heart ached. To steady himself, he pressed the center of his chest with his fist. The computer screen showed a photograph of him in the matching vest and hat.

His chest hurt all the way through to his spine.

Tonight, Maurice was just tired, so his pain was dull, and he looked out of his Bronx apartment window and saw the lights coming on nearby and as far as the skyscrapers in Manhattan.

There were thousands of bright windows. Each one glowed with electricity. In each apartment, someone flipped on the switch, and the light came on because two hot wires contacted one another. Watching the lights now, Maurice felt that his father was wrong.

There was only one woman for each man. Myra was his flame, his match. They had burned bright.

The Empire State Building glowed in the distance.

Maurice now passed it many times while making deliveries. Sometimes, he circled its base and filtered in and out of the nearby buildings like a moth under a lamp. But he had never been to the top, and he knew that he wouldn't.

He tried to think about tomorrow—delivering packages, going from door to door, looking for the exits, greeting more people.

But that was impossible. So Maurice stared out of the window and watched all the lights until one by one they went dark.

The One that Did Not Get Away

My boyfriend refuses to tell me where he got the scar on his face.

"It's from fishing," he says.

"It's from some war," I suggest.

His profile is charming like one of those men who would stand calmly in the midst of burning rockets and order an attack.

"It's from casting too far out," he says. "A hook getting caught in my neck."

"It's from a night in the moat trying to save a damsel in distress," I joke. I try to jolly him. Maybe if he's caught unaware, he will blurt it out. It's such a fine scar traveling from below the chin to the front of his ear like a slow passionate kiss. At various points, the scar makes little snags and bursts.

It is keloid. Tissue never healed over the cut so now it appears shiny and reflective against the mat of his face.

"It looks like lightning against the black of the sky," I tell him.

He bows his head, smiles and kisses my hand. He says he admires my sense of poetry.

I think that's what brought us together—my poetic spirit and his mystery to me.

He is very handsome and kind in the way of Southern gentlemen. He is also very humble and noble. "Simple," is how he calls himself.

"No," I tell him, "You are too fast for the average person to recognize, much, much too adventurous. By the way, where did you get that scar?"

"In a sinking boat," he answers.

Maybe this is a clue.

Men are like that in New Orleans and possibly the world. From what I've seen they will not tell you the truth. They couch themselves in our overwrought lives—women's that is. On our brocade couches, men languor and bathe silently, handsomely, and romantically while we must figure them out. "What to do with the man?" we concentrate.

In my girlhood and my womanhood, I look for a mate. I must find him from his disguises of masculinity. It is the Southern tradition. They chase. We pray.

In the cathedral, I sit with my girlfriend. In the diffracted, prismatic, stained-glass light, under our veils, in the shadows, we whisper our hopes.

"He is dangerous," my friend says.

We live in the small parts of New Orleans. In the Catholic, feminine, and familial territories where all is known. We tell stories. We sit on porches and near sickbeds. We gather in churches and bingo parlors. We make our own entertainment.

There is a big tree down by the river where we picnic with distant cousins and men from our past like uncles and fathers. They talk big and brag. We laugh lightly. We flirt. We practice our feminine wiles and hone our traditions of desire. We pray for the right men to come along.

In my young life, everything was so plain. Up too early in the morning for school. Come home to find Mama cooking. Papa on his way out to get drunk.

My boyfriend is the first man I have met who has mystery. He has excitement, a past I don't know and a scar as proof of his difference.

"Looks like your Papa when he was a boy," Mama likes to relate everything. She wants all the same from past to present to the times beyond.

But it is my life ahead. I am old enough to see what has gone before me was wasted. Sixteen years I already spent without harpooning romance, without waltzing desire, without fulfillment. I have never been fought over under the Dueling Oaks. I have never been kissed on the levee and then held hands in suicidal duet and plunged into the river. I have never lived in a bordello or run with pirates, even though this is New Orleans.

It is my privilege now to have finally met a man with a scar. Not a deep scar, a fine scar. One that gives character to him and excitement to me—the plain, the sheltered, and the unadventured.

I will change. We are going to change my life. I will rise from my knees, throw off my veil, and pierce my ears. I will marry a man with a scar.

"Should I really worry about where you got it?" I tease.

"Back of Lake Borgne."

I laugh.

Lake Borgne is a little rural fork in the water between high mosquito grass where shrimpers and other lonely men go. They start out early in the morning when the only light they see is from their own kerosene lamps. They come home smelling like swamp, and fall tired and drunk into their beds at night.

"Lake Borgne," I laugh. "That sounds like an old man's fish tale."

The nights will be unimportant to me until he and I see them together, beginning the evening we are married. "We will elope. We will ride in a horse-drawn carriage through the jasmine streets. We will pass the cathedral to make the sign of the cross," I place one finger on the side of his neck when I tell him. I trace the line of his scar, our scar, following it right up to the ear, then independently, I go around.

"Are you listening?" I moisten my finger with a kiss so it will feel sweet and soft, "if you will not tell me where you got this scar, about your past, I will not tell you about our future. Don't you want to know?"

He nods.

"We will live in a little white house," I tell him.

"Near Lake Borgne," he says.

"We will sleep on a bed of down and moss. We will not get home until dawn on the night of our elopement from drinking champagne and dancing the waltz. We will arrive at our door when the peach of the rising sun tints the morning onto our wedding white clothes. And only then will we make passionate love. And only then will we sleep," I take his hand.

He studies the lines of my palms, first the left and then the right before he places them together and closed. Then he envelopes my hands with his own.

"We will get home at dawn," he repeats, "Dawn? What month?"

"June, of course."

"Good. Then they ought to be running trout."

Sometimes I feel like he is not listening to me. But men make such pretenses. They claim their muscles are a sign of their strength. They brag their eyes are not the windows to their souls. They tell each other that together they could win such things as wars, when wars are won by ideas and deals, no matter the number of dead. We will be married in wedding white, whether he hears it or not.

The dress I plan for elopement is sheer and pure, cut from the mid-bolt of the cloth. It has no dirty ends of flaws running first one wrong direction then another. The holes of the weave are very small and sturdier than mosquito net, and the fabric glows new and white like a lantern guiding a skiff in the dark. It will be a beacon for the beginning of my life, a last reflection on all of us.

My girlfriend and I, we maidens, demonstrate our breeding through such simplicity. Our knees never show below the hems of our dresses. The shoulders of our boat collars never quite slide off. Our hair obeys nights of meticulous training to stay on our necks or behind the ear. Just about the place where my boyfriend's scar begins, on me a wiry branch from my scalp threatens to jump out. I will let it go, once I am wed. I will start to be dangerous.

"The scissors," my girlfriend hands me the implement for making my entrance. The elopement dress has been sewn askew. I rip open a seam. The front and back fly open easily and silently like skin willing to part.

"Catch it."

My girlfriend lays out her arms for the pieces of cloth while I rethink the construction. It should be straight. The stitches should not show to anyone else. Only I will know how they got there.

"That scar," I asked him once, "has anyone told you about it? Do they ask why it never went away?"

"It's in my blood, I guess." He has inherited the factors of clotting and unclotting himself, the skin that heals, but does not bind over, the genes for keeping infection at bay.

This scar is a sign of his health, his fighting spirit, his eternal resistance. It will be mine when we are married, this wound against even the body's conventions.

My girlfriend puts the needle back into the seam.

She memorizes for me the last night I will be among them. She promises to tell everyone.

"I will say that you reached the cathedral at midnight," she takes a ricochet stitch, "And that he looked only into your eyes."

"Tell them that he wanted to take me then. But I refused."

109

She blushes.

"Tell them that I said first when and where we made love," I remind.

Back of Lake Borgne it has already happened. But it was not sin. It was more like a miracle, the saint descending onto the flowers and blessing them, changing their colors from white to red, in abundance, profoundness and silence. Then gone. Nothing remained but the reeds flattened, the roses, an overripe smell tainting the air.

Nobody knows but me, not even him. He claims I was not there. "Still a virgin," he tells everybody.

Once I saw him unhook a fish. He had to take the metal prongs out through the same holes that they entered. He held it still, his hands firm against the open jaws. There was a kindness in his making it immobile. The fish swung and shivered from its tail to its chest. Finally it submitted. The hook came out with a slight bit of flesh on it, and even the bait came out again. Then he tossed the fish into the ice chest. There was one sound of flop, then writhing, then grating, then stillness.

I swim not far from Lake Borgne, in the Intracoastal Canal where there is sometimes dangerous water. You can see whirlpools if you stand in the rocking boat. But you cannot when they are level with your head. You only feel little tugs at your arms, legs, and hair as if you were caught but not yet drowning. It can be exciting and pleasant like getting caught in a school of mullet.

"Men enter marriage with their eyes closed," my Mama said. Is it true? They come in from the blind, dark side of the church. They wait with lips dry and mind suspended, swimming into the unknown. Sometimes I wonder, "Do I?"

I wriggled the hook at my boyfriend, the day he took off the fish. "With this," I said, "I'm going to get you."

He took it out of my hand, stuck on a worm, and dropped it back into the water, "Don't play." I fear he meant it.

It was a sullen afternoon when we came home. It was smelly, and cloudy, and dark. We dropped the bait and the ice in the side of the grass at the shore to feed the fish we had not caught, to proliferate the species. Then we pulled up the boat.

His arms turning the crank assured me. His body was something into which I could merge. The muscles could be taken apart bit by bit, dived through, fileted. Then in the open, bare bones of himself, he would know he would really want me.

"Do I put words in your mouth?" once I asked him.

"Nothing much else goes in there."

He was eating a sandwich, drinking a beer, and tossing the pickle up in the air to catch it like a fish snapping a fly. Full, open mouth, he grinned.

I felt like slicing him just at the moment. Taking the knife from the table and running it, serrated and all, just above the line of his scar. "Take me seriously," I wanted to say. But I didn't. I was still unsure then whether he would take me at all.

That night it happened. The first love on the banks. The moonlight, the moored rocking boat, the reeds, the sounds of insects, and splashing. The saint descending just for me. We were for each other, were we not, in our virginal pre-nuptial paring?

Each of my uncles and brothers and cousins, each of them fathers, has said, "Never." Then one by one, I heard from the girlfriends, mothers, and wives that they were the love makers. They made the love, the women, long before marriage. "Love is a powerful thing." They hand me this secret like they would pass me the candle or give me the dust. They cup my palm with theirs, make a pocket that is empty, and they said the invisible word, "Love."

"It is love," they nod over my boyfriend's glazed eyes, and they see the line caught from his mind to his heart. They tell me, "You are safe." These are powerful women.

We all picnic by the river. Women and men. We spread the blankets, toss the balls, babble to babies, cuddle the children.

We break into our separate domains, women near the food and the tables, men by the cars, parked up on the grass, talking loudly and drinking.

It is not by force that we get together. It is not by accident. It is not by aberration. It is not bait, prayer, flirtation, aphrodisiac, mojo, root. It is love. I have been well trained.

"What will you do on our wedding night," I ask my boyfriend, "the night after we are married? Will we honeymoon well? Will we stay in the chambers?"

"I'm thinking of going out to fish. That's how I make my living."

His head is turned and his profile is straight, a flat, dark shadow from his lowered temple to his high chest. He is almost invisible with the night all around him, around us. I feel I must turn this corner, get to the other side of his face, where the scar sits in all its contentedness.

"I don't think you love me. I don't think you want me. I'm just something else that you caught," I suggest.

A thought splashes above his brow for a moment before he responds, "Do you want to be an old fisherman's wife, to be the wife of a scar-faced, sometimes drunk?"

I recognize a proposal when I hear one at last,

"Yes." I answer, "Yes. Yes."

I have looked for this wedding all of my life, at least the part I can remember. Before that, I tumbled aimlessly, playing the rolling games of babies, winding in my mother's stomach, floating like a piece of dry bark on water.

Before dresses and boyfriends, and smiles for uncles and Papa, before I knew up and down, north and south, when there was only me, I seem to remember there was nothing at all. There was nothing asked and nothing given. There was no want or fear or even love. There was no destiny.

The destination began with my girlhood and a need to make everything right in the world. These chores were left by earlier generations. Mothers whispered, it was men who gave women meaning: To understand and forgive them, to carry their secrets, to uphold their spirits. Women bore these as love—heavy and clumsy, and sometimes hurtful and weak.

I was predestined because of my fault, my fissure, my actual femininity that increasingly had to be covered over, hidden and prided, laced and decorated, paraded and used.

I told my boyfriend once that I have a scar, but it bleeds every month, just like the stigmata or the weeping heart of Jesus.

"Don't make blasphemy," he said and he did not touch me for a long, long time after that.

I went fishing once alone. I pressed myself into the morning darkness between endless lake and sky where stepping off shore was an act of sound rather than sight.

Like the young men, the old men and the old women who sometimes grow moustaches and wear hats tacked down to their heads with leftover scarves, I sat in a barely rocking boat. I wondered, "Is this complete freedom?"

My girlfriend and I covered our heads in church for many years before the invention of the chapel veil. It looked like a lace pie plate or the kind of scrap you might put under a vase over the wooden sideboard to protect it from bruising.

The invention of the chapel veil meant that it could be carried in the pocketbook, along with the rain bonnet. It could be secured by the metal bob pin. It could be recognized by the church as covering the head without compromising the hair.

We wore the chapel veil for a while. But it always seemed odd. Our problem was that we prayed in the cathedral. We knelt in the elegant half-light, under the ornate, iron-encased glass, amid the gold furnishings, before the silk vestments. The chapel veil did not fit. We returned to the mantilla.

The baby inside me grows like a minnow. I dream of fish, reeling them close, showing them off. I tell no one, especially him, of my condition. He may not want to get married. Perhaps, he will find me distastefully large, too importantly fat.

"Let us concede to abandon," I suggest to him. "Be wed without vestments, run off without the trappings of romance."

I ask him again, "Do you want to get shotgun married? Make back seat magic? Jump a broom? Buy a six pack?"

He is convinced.

The wedding pictures that were not taken, no one is surprised not to see.

"Look at my album," the women in the family call, for the first time pulling out books with torn and blank pages. "Here is when I was a girl. There is where I was wed. This is childbirth."

They look at me.

I blame no one for my mistakes, I explain. I look at the ground. I do not see my feet.

My girlfriend puts the elopement dress next to me.

"Still fits," she says.

I disagree. If we travel the seams below the arms we will notice that the fabric won't stretch, that my shape is more woman, that I have grown emphatically.

My girlfriend says she will save the dress for my daughter. "Perhaps she will have what you can't."

"It's no longer important. It's far too tame an end. It's not even scary, much less the measure of danger." I lie. Instead, I say, "Please don't."

When I lay in bed, I convince my husband that I see not one difference between marrying him under the guise of romantic attachment or under the guidance of rush. Partly, it's true that the end is the same while only the means are deflowered. That isn't difference enough.

That night, a dream brings my husband to the side of my hospital bed. I have just given birth.

"Where is my child?" I ask.

"She is swimming in the Intracoastal Canal. She is boarding a trawl in Lake Pontchartrain at the corner of Elysian Fields Avenue. She is too small, too weak, too skimpy, too female," he says, "I threw her back."

I scream myself awake.

I turn to my husband, "How can I allow my daughter the dreams of a girl without taking a woman's hard life? Must she see but not lead, guide but not speak, and hope against reality?"

"That's not a question," my husband responds. He quickly goes back to sleep.

"What do you know?" I respond. "You have been visibly scarred. Now stay safe," I curse. "Keep your small aspirations."

He breathes shallow and soft, like swimming on course. He has been, he once said, since he met me.

I pray in the alcove that shelters the Virgin. Mothers here rise up from the kneelers, brushing down trails of electricity that have risen and traveled the center aisle of their skirts. They lift flimsy material from big, sweaty legs, sit to rub the red impressions of bones that come through to their skin before walking outside to the street. This is the only clue to the neighbors that something may hurt.

The Virgin, for us much more than plaster, stands patient and placid as symbol, but shares our pain. She knows our heartaches—to begin womanhood early, to steady the world, to have a secret self far different from her earthly condition.

As we stand, woman and girls, or sit in prayer or in loathing outside of the church, we have so many doubts, but there is no place for our fear. No saint is the model of misstep or weakness. Heaven must be ideal.

Along cathedral corridors of chipped stone by rough hand, we pass fountains of blessed water and statues whose bare feet we touch lightly with whispered petition. There is no niche for confusion, misinformation, mispurpose.

There is no crèche for a rest.

When my husband comes into my bed in the evenings, he moves now in ways I know, not for their blessedness nor for their freeing. The scar on his face shines like my road map.

The Prayers of the Sycophant*
(*accuser of fig thieves)

Again this summer, the fig tree in Sharon's yard reached over the fence and dropped fruit, too much fruit, next door. Fat, magenta, perfectly formed pendant figs with sweet, pink, seedy insides. There were so many left on the ground in her neighbor's yard that it looked like a dusty corral with the exception of one corner, which was covered with a dark Persian carpet of smashed pink circles and overripe purple hearts. Her hearts.

She stood in the open screen door at the back of her house and stared unforgivingly at the rotting fruit. She considered the ways that she had tried to convince the neighbor children, the parties responsible for running the once-verdant yard to dirt, that they should pick up the figs as soon as they dropped, put them in a basket—or barring a basket, a bucket—and bring them inside to their mother who could wash and give them figs for dessert.

"Look boys, figs are a delicious fruit," she had called to them.

She named them collectively "boys" because she didn't

know one from another. Their ages appeared to be so close. They were uniformly skinny and grimy. They passed clothes back and forth so that Monday a tall one would wear high-water jeans, and Tuesday a short one would have on the jeans with deep folded cuffs. She recognized the same jeans by the torn pockets.

A while back, she had attempted to learn the boys' names but that had turned out badly.

"Hello Errol," she said.

"I'm Jacques."

"So sorry. Where is your brother?"

"Why you want to know?"

"No reason."

"Then, why you ask?"

"Courtesy."

The boy gave her a confused look then walked away while she remained at the screen door with a frozen smile.

The next time she used the collective nomenclature.

"Boys," she had said biting into the fig as demonstration. "See how the fig is soft inside."

"Euuu," they said together.

One picked up a fig and smashed it between his fingers. He pushed the pulp into another's face. Then the others reached down quickly into the carpet of figs and took the sweetest, overripe fruit and used them as missiles. They threw figs with such energy and poor aim that the back of their white wooden house sported pink, oddly-formed polka dots as if someone killed giant blood-filled mosquitos against the outside wall. The juice from the splattered figs brought the flies to the back door, then the wasps. They emerged from mud cocoons under the eaves of the building and lighted on the dots, the shattered fruit, then the children. They went screaming into their house, slamming the screen door behind them.

"Ain't I told y'all not to run in here. Now sit your asses down and be quiet."

118

The mother's voice echoed in the quiet afternoon of the neighborhood.

Sharon stood in the back door holding her half-eaten fig.

"What a waste," she said aloud, half-hoping someone would hear and take umbrage.

She had meant the figs, the children, and the dysfunctional family. They were so typical of the nomadic people who now breeched her neighborhood. They came—usually at twilight—with big families and little furniture. Then they spent the first evening on the porch talking loudly and eating food that at least one of them would fail to pick up before morning.

They were cultivators of mice, roaches, and fleas if they brought the pit bulls with them for protection. And after causing havoc, they'd move out anywhere from six months to a year.

She knew the routine, even the part where their landlord apologized. "I'm having a hard time renting the place," he said. "The section 8 pays three times the real rent."

"I know," she answered, "It's not fair." But she never told the landlord the exact cause of her discomfort.

Her efforts and that of several other young, white, Northern urbanites had prodded this old neighborhood to life. Marginal when she moved in years before the storm, the place had become habitable and trendy.

The Times-Picayune even came out and took a picture of her pink, blue, and green painted home. And soon afterwards, the value of the housing stock increased. But then, the city declared its experiment in mixed-use housing: The projects were torn down, their unsavory residents scattered to neighborhoods like hers and the free-for-all began.

That's when landlords profited. The section 8s profited. And everyone had made out except her. Sharon worried about the property values. Her husband Richard noted that poor people populated the neighborhood long before she moved to New Orleans, "They were here first."

"So were the Indians," she responded. "Let's give them the French Quarter."

At one time, he would have thought she was funny. Now, he looked at her and sighed. He seemed to perceive all of her comments these days as too serious.

And maybe her sense of humor had waned since the children next door had moved in, trampling brown paths through the St. Augustine grass and ignoring Sharon's suggestions to pick up the paper trash in front of their door.

Her face had become more dry and rutted between her brows. The lines around her mouth that once marked laughter now ran to her chin with disappointment. The thin fingers that Richard used to hold often now busied themselves with yard work.

"We have the two of us," he said and hugged her as if that were a good thing.

At the time, she yielded, feeling that her opportunities were still coming.

The other young couples who had helped remake the neighborhood had quickly conceived children, sold their renovated homes, and moved out to the suburbs. Their hefty profits bought them more room, driveways, and modern conveniences.

Richard was among the first to paint the old house, put up a picket fence, install walkway lights, and trim around the garden. When he became tired and out of breath, Sharon had planted the perennials that complimented the ancient shrubs and century-old oak trees. Now, the curb sported nascent throngs of pink and green elephant ears. The area around the fence had adolescent crepe myrtles, and the middle of the yard held a rope swing from the ancient weeping willow. Everything grew because of the distribution of sunlight, the daily outpouring of thunderstorms, and the comforting embrace of humidity. Sharon had believed that the fertility of the neighborhood could still extend to her.

She left the screen door and turned toward the inside of the house, becoming slightly blind from suddenly going from the daylight into the darkness. She felt her way through the kitchen and toward the bedroom by reading the braille of the unfinished linoleum with her bare feet.

Richard had prodded her to come from New York and live with him in New Orleans.

"It'll be an adventure in Southern culture, living. Think botany."

He reached her soft spot by saying the word that fueled her imagination. She loved edible plants, amateur science, and the environment.

She planted bay leaf (laurus nobilis), cayenne peppers (capsicum frutescens), and Creole tomatoes (which she couldn't find in Latin.)

She came because of her love of culinary vocabulary but mostly because of Richard's passion for his hometown. There were empty houses and empty lots. She and Richard could fill the spaces.

They unpacked a van full of boxes with her clothing and small packages of seeds that she had collected for the fruit and vegetable patches.

But the prize was already there. The fig tree must have been 50 years old. The trunk was as thick as a telephone pole. It was ashy white with big nubs where it had been trimmed back. Still, she couldn't understand why the owners had cut the lower branches so frequently, making the tree so tall that she had to get a ladder to pick the fruit and, worse, why had it been pruned so lopsidedly that the fruit fell mostly in her neighbor's yard.

Sharon had tried to even the odds when she first moved in by asking her neighbor to swap: If the old lady—living there at the time—gave Sharon the fruit that dropped so prolifically, she would make fig scones or even return a jar of fig preserves.

But the old lady wouldn't hear of it. Literally, she was half-deaf. "You want to give me stones? What kind of stones? Pig stones?"

Sharon didn't even try to explain it. She just politely backed away. The next day, she handed the woman a scone wrapped in a white, monogrammed-cloth napkin she brought at a vintage-wares store.

"When she saw the woman again, she asked, "Did you like the pastry?"

"That was pretty," the old woman answered, "But don't give me no more of them biscuits. Dry, dry, dry."

Sharon tried to tell Richard about the old woman's rudeness. But he wouldn't hear of it. "You don't understand people," he said.

"That certainly makes me feel better," she answered.

She still secretly maintained that she could get the old lady to properly utilize the figs. Sharon studied nouvelle cuisine Louisiana recipes—fig jelly, fig butter, fig-pepper soup. She planned to offer her neighbor gourmet meals made with local ingredients.

But before she could bring the next plate, the old lady died.

Sharon eyed the empty back yard for a week. Then, one night she could stand it no more. She grabbed a pillowcase and snuck down her neighbor's alley.

She filled the pillowcase with fallen figs and ran back to her house. Only the pillowcase disclosed her theft. Its maroon stains wouldn't wash out.

Not long after that, the Section 8s moved in.

They had more children than furniture. More furniture than tableware. Paper plates and food boxes washed against her fence. Their voices drowned out her classical music at breakfast. Someone— it seemed many of them—was learning the trumpet.

When she complained to Richard, he told her, "Welcome to New Orleans." He kissed her on the forehead and left for the peaceful environment of his job.

Sharon spent her days digging, pulling, separating, pruning, and cutting the garden to encourage new growth.

But life became increasingly unmanageable when her doctor called to say that his treatments didn't work. She was not pregnant. He suggested that $12,000 wasn't enough. "The embryos don't always take."

Sharon hung up.

"We should sue," Sharon told Richard that night. They had already invested in boosting his sperm, thickening her blood, investigating his arrhythmias, and pacing her menstrual clock.

"Sue who? The doctor or God?" he responded.

If he was trying to be funny, she didn't laugh.

She went to the back door now and looked at the fig tree. The ends of the long branches hung heavy with ripe fruit. Even the birds had gotten some. They made deep pits into the otherwise perfect figs as if bullets had exploded bald, dark heads and exposed the pink matter of brains.

Sharon had once figured a way to save the fruit before it became ruined by feathered pillagers. She purchased two long-handled canes sold on television to help the elderly retrieve items from high shelves. The canes had pincers at one end and a squeeze handle at the other. One night when her neighbors were asleep and Richard was working late, she leaned a wooden ladder against the fence, carried the two canes up mid-way on the rungs and leaned over to the next yard. The tongs of one cane held a bag while the tongs of the other cane picked figs. She balanced a flashlight on one of the rungs to spotlight the low branches.

But almost every time that she picked, a ripe piece of fruit fell into the dirt, not in the bag. She knew the figs would just lay there and rot. It was almost as if the figs didn't want to be saved, she thought momentarily. Just as quickly, she realized that was a crazy idea. Her intentions were flawless, even if her execution wasn't.

Then, she saw the light come on in her house and Richard called her name. At first, she was too embarrassed to answer. What would she say, "I'm in the yard in the dark trying to rescue figs?" She suddenly felt ridiculous.

She tried to rush down the ladder. But the flashlight fell off first. She was now in total darkness. She dropped one of the canes on the ground in the next door yard. Then she tore her blouse on the top of the fence. Her stash of figs tipped over. She felt them squash under her feet as she finally made her way off the ladder and rushed toward the back door. But by the time she got to the house and ran to the front, Richard, not finding her, had gone out.

Sharon looked at the purple trail of pulp that her shoes carried from the yard. She was too proud to call him on his cell phone.

She had returned the ladder to the shed and found a space for the cane and the bag. She cleaned her shoes, dropped her torn blouse into the laundry basket, and mopped the purple-mottled floor.

By the time Richard returned, the house was clean and the food put away except for a plate kept for him in the microwave.

She had slipped on a pale purple nighty and displayed the figs that she gathered in a green porcelain Chinese vase. Sitting on a bed of fizzy grape leaves were three purple figs, a small but bountiful nuclear family.

Richard didn't notice the display as he headed from the front door to the bathroom. "It's true that you can't buy beer, you can only rent it." He laughed at the old joke.

Sharon heard his urine splashing as he called to her, "Where were you earlier?

"Just out in the neighborhood," she answered.

"Good, you're finally circulating."

"Yeah," she grimaced as he exited the room without flushing. He saw the look and returned, "Sorry."

His apology gave her no satisfaction.

When Sharon married Richard, she loved that he was a neighbor to everyone. Now, his behavior worried her. Why wasn't he home making a family? It seemed as if his lack of enthusiasm had caused her barrenness.

Richard had always talked to the people in the neighborhood, but now she sensed him turning into one of them. He still hung out at the bar with the neon sign on the corner where he frequently had after-work beers with the other homeowners. He once sat around talking with the homeowners and their plasterers, painters and plumbers—all the guys. They were a nice group—the men who came to renovate the old houses and the men whose families had been working in the neighborhood for centuries. They were all decent people.

But then the new people moved in, and Richard kept the same habits. These men smoked cigarettes on the corner and sat on their steps in the daytime. They waved inconsistently—sometimes they smiled, overjoyed, it seemed to see her. And other times, they ignored her and kept their heads in their hands.

Sharon sometimes watched from her front porch as the men grasped one another in bear hugs. Then other men, who were not neighbors at all, came in and out of the neighborhood. They drove very, very expensive cars. If they stopped at the bar, they stayed for only a short time, said hello to everyone, then left.

She asked Richard, "Are they drug dealers?"

"Don't be ridiculous."

It was the first time that he had made her question herself.

She couldn't trust Richard completely on this one. He didn't make distinctions among people, and he always wanted to be one of the boys. They did not tell their wives everything, especially if they thought the information would worry them.

But she wasn't afraid of drug dealers—not the little guys anyway. All of them, all the new urbanites, "Urban Unites," as they had once referred to their little alcove of Northern pioneers, had sold a little reefer in college, done a taste of coke, sometimes did ecstasy or mushrooms, and they had learned from it—too expensive, too distracting, too dangerous. So they had sipped wine on Sunday afternoons together and occasionally drank margaritas or other decorative cocktails just for a laugh.

But now, the Urban Unites were gone with their good intentions, and the neighborhood had changed. Sharon started to see a fellow with low hanging pants and dreadlocks sitting on her steps with Richard or Richard sitting on one of the neighbor's steps with him.

"And he is . . . ," she asked Richard in a way that made her sound cool and not overly wifely, she thought.

"Just a friend," he said.

Sharon did not respond. Not outwardly.

She began to wonder. Even a little marijuana might throw the treatments off.

At first, Sharon mollified her worries by secretly calling Richard's new friend "the Jamaican," a name that gave him a little caché. Then, she decided that at some point, she'd ask Richard if he had started smoking again and what was he thinking. But she didn't.

She should have examined whether his eyes were more than tired, and asked if someone else's cigarette smoke was in his hair. She should have asked. Or she should have known and done something.

Instead, she gardened.

She placed her hands of the warm soil, felt for rocks with her fingers. She pushed them aside to make the soil good for planting. Then she cupped her hands into a shovel and made a place for the seeds. She sprinkled seeds that looked like wood shavings, others that looked like slivers of hay, and some flatter and smaller than grains of rice. Everything could be eaten or would make their lives more beautiful.

It was "the Jamaican" who brought Richard home the night that his head hurt.

"The Jamaican" was not a friend. All of their nearest friends had moved on. And the few times that they returned to visit, their children ran amuck in the yard. They picked Sharon's rhododendron and trampled her elephant ears.

"Aren't you glad we don't have that problem?" Richard asked her when the visitors left.

She held him tight knowing that he knew the answer.

The doorbell woke her from her daydreams.

A few of the "boys" stood on her front porch.

"Miss, he say, when you going to come back outside? We seen you at the back door. My cousin, he want to ask you something."

Sharon looked through the screen at the dusty hoard outside of her door.

"What does he want?" she said and peered for a face in the group who looked like the enquirer.

"He ain't with us. He in the kitchen now. He say when you come to the back door, he want to ask you something."

"Well, wait just a minute." She left the inner door open but made sure there was no inviting crack in the screen. She returned to the bedroom for one more moment to herself. She saw Richard's shirt on the floor of the opened closet. It was the shirt he was wearing when he came home alone for the last time. Why hadn't she spoken to him earlier?

She put the plaid, musty fabric to her nose and inhaled. Salt. Sweat. House paint. The musk of him. He was a tall, strong man with good arms, a good smile, good genes, a vulnerable heart.

The rest of his clothes were long gone. First gone were the clothes that she left at the hospital. The staff there had handed them to her in a plastic bag. She dropped it into the garbage just before she walked slowly out of the automatic reflecting, glass doors into the night.

She had arrived like lightning into the emergency room corridor.

She raced from the ambulance dock at the emergency room through the long halls to the admitting office, screaming at the attendants, maybe screaming, they told her screaming. She was just trying to get her point across.

"He's talking out of his head," she grabbed a nurse by the arm who gave her an awful, evil look.

"He doesn't recognize me! He doesn't know who I am!"

The nurse said, "Sit here and someone will be out for you in a minute."

Sharon sat in a nearby, crowded room and looked all around. There were people slumped in chairs, holding their heads or their bleeding arms. There were people lying stretched impossibly over two metal armchairs. There was a woman whose child was limp, shiny, and flushed. The mother ran a wet cloth over the child's face and neck.

She heard the sharp voices of doctors approaching in the hall, and she rose slightly to greet them. But they walked quickly past the open door of the waiting room to a separate area.

"Gunshot," she heard one of the orderlies say to them in the hallway.

Then, a stretcher, doctors and nurses filled the hallway and passed in a clot to another inner room.

Sharon returned to the emergency room attendant's desk.

"Can I at least see my husband?" Sharon said.

"No, Mam. We can't do that. Too many people in here tonight. Some very bad," the woman at the desk said.

"That's outrageous!" Sharon replied.

The woman picked up the phone and turned her head.

Sharon thought of breaking through the nearby blank double doors where all the stretchers had passed, but that wouldn't help Richard's case any. So she sat, closed her eyes, and tried to put into words the way she found him so that she could finally tell the doctors.

Richard had stumbled into the front room of their home, supported by "the Jamaican."

He said, "See you, bro."

Then, he put Richard in Sharon's arms.

But Richard could hardly stand and, almost as soon as the door closed, he and Sharon toppled over, on to the floor.

Then, Richard threw up.

"Hey, what's wrong with you?" Sharon asked, "Drunk?"

She was joking and patting his cheek with her hand. But he didn't respond.

"OK, baby. You've got to get up now or I'll have to call the doctor." Then, she saw his eyes open, roll back in his head.

"Oh my God," she ran to the door to look for the man who had brought Richard inside. "What did you do to him?" she hollered down the empty street.

"Oh God. Oh God." She went to the phone and dialed 911. The ambulance came 15 minutes later. By then Richard was talking out of his head.

At least he was talking. But his eyes were open and he didn't know her.

"My God, my God, my God, Richard," Sharon sat by his side until the ambulance came and they loaded him in. They wouldn't let her ride, and she didn't protest because that would just delay them further. So she grabbed her purse, jumped in the car, and may have left the front door open.

A few of the people on her block came out. She could see their curious glances as she got in the car.

"Everything OK, Miss?" one of them asked.

"Of course not," she shouted back.

At the hospital, a nurse told her, "Probably overdose."

"Overdose of what? How? Richard doesn't do drugs."

"He smelled like marijuana, and they're putting a lot of PCP and other additives in that lately. He had all the symptoms of PCP poisoning—racing heart, high blood pressure. Or it could just be an everyday stroke."

"Can't you do an autopsy?" Sharon asked.

The nurse looked at Sharon as if she had three heads. "He will get an autopsy if you want to wait that long. The doctors are extremely busy. So is the coroner."

"There may have been foul play," Sharon heard her voice rising outside of herself.

"There always is," the woman answered flatly. Then her tone changed, but just for a moment. "I'm very sorry about your loss. You can't believe the loss we see here every day. If it was my husband, I'd just want him buried."

But it was more than loss. It was murder. Sharon emailed the hospital, talked to the police, to the neighbors, to the guys. Everybody who knew Richard said it was not his fault. But no one would help. They said they'd have to accuse too many people.

Still, she didn't trust them. They were accustomed to their powerlessness and the lazy, bloated justice system. They would never help her find "the friend" who brought Richard home even though she thought she saw him everywhere—among all the dropped pants, dreadlocked boys who populated nearby streets and grocery stores, not just in her neighborhood but all over the city. She was just never sure which one was "the Jamaican," the name that once had caché but now named Richard's murderer.

Sharon stood at the door often now, thinking that one day he would return to the street. She'd peer at the neighborhood bar from her window. One day she would have him arrested.

There was another reason she stayed. She couldn't move. She couldn't recoup the money that Richard and she had put into the house because now there were bad neighbors who were running down the neighborhood.

And as for their children. They covered the street, running and shouting, and making so much unnecessary noise. She got in the habit of putting her fingers inside her ears and closing her eyes as she stood at the window.

If she had had children, they would have been nothing like her neighbors' hordes. Carrying on in the yard, crying on the step, and getting bigger every day. To what purpose?

First, she and Richard never would have stayed on this block. They would have moved to someplace in the suburbs where there were people like them. They could have had their house, their lawn, their clean, square rooms with plumb corners and crown molding, their intercom where they could listen to their own children playing from the other room while they relaxed with one another—doing whatever they wanted in the safety of their home.

But she was stuck, now with this low life, in this low life, which pitched off course in every direction.

The doorbell rang again.

"What, goddammit?" she went to the door. She opened it and there he was. The man who killed Richard. "Oh, God," she said. She raced to her cell phone to call the police.

While she was dialing, he walked into her house, and she screamed. "Get out! Get out! Murderer!"

He reached for her as she hollered into the phone, "Help."

He took the phone from her hand, "Miss. Miss, stop."

She pushed him away.

He stood back. His face was soft with disappointment. "I was just trying to say sorry about your husband. You remember me? I found him on the sidewalk that day and I brought him home. I'm the one. Remember me? I'm the one who picked him up and brought him home."

Sharon stopped breathing and looked toward him. Everything about him should have said murderer. But she could see now that he wasn't.

He was just a boy, a bigger boy like all the boys standing in her front room looking frightened.

She knew it, and she had to accept it.

The boys, all the boys, dirty, unkempt and trembling stood together in her front room. They were watching her with big eyes, but as if she was the one to be pitied.

The smallest one moved forward to grab his cousin's hand and pulled him toward the door.

Sharon stood mute.

"Let's go y'all," the tall, dreadlocked cousin turned and walked out of the house herding the children with him. He left Sharon there, standing alone where she had last seen Richard alive.

She had taken Richard in her arms, and they had fallen, fallen through no fault of their own. They had done nothing so bad to deserve this. That was her worse realization of all.

"Why God?" she asked a question only He could answer.

But there was too much commotion in the neighbors' house—laughter, cursing, the voices of people gambling, and the children crying and calling one another— that she could not hear herself think. And she could not hear the voice of God telling her to listen. She stayed on her knees and begged as the sun fell and the figs fell and the juice seeped from the rotting fruit like the very nature of injustice.

Leo Walks Home

L eo threw his right leg forward, then his left leg, and moved slowly on the sidewalk toward his house as he had for the last 40 years. He had recovered from childhood polio, but he clearly remembered the years when he was crippled. He had lain in bed, swathed in covers, actually watching the grass grow in the empty lot next door.

In the summer, the weeds rose fast and seedy. If Mr. Biennami didn't arrive with the rattling push mower every week, the frogs and snakes would nest in the grass. Then, the next time he came, he would need to wear his pants tucked into his socks so that nothing would bite him as he wielded the long-handled sickle.

Once Mr. Biennami stuck an innocent green creature whose appendages flew up limp while blood scattered. Mr. Biennami glanced up at Leo, watching from the window, and shrugged.

In the fall, Leo watched the boys from the neighborhood play with the soft leather football. They banged into one another so hard that once Big Michael lost a tooth. He laughed and put it in his pocket.

Then the others howled with him, patted one another on the back, and resumed their play.

In the winter, it was just Leo and the window. The lot next door looked swampy and wet. There was little to see because the cold discouraged the fireflies in the evening. But if Leo woke extra early and inched his body across the bed to his watching spot, he saw a haze of fog sitting like a halo on the grass. His mother said heaven was trying to get closer to him. He didn't know whether she said that to cheer him or prepare him for death. So he smiled when she was nearby. But he worried when she left the room. He thanked God every day in the winter that he woke up.

Spring came and he was still there. The grass had a greener smell. The honey-perfumed jasmine blossomed and so did the tart, early gardenias. He could keep his eyes closed and, even half-asleep, he felt life around him.

Then, he was scheduled for surgery. It was risky for a boy in those years. The white doctors who took on his case at Charity Hospital were very kind. Perhaps it was because the black doctors from his neighborhood frequently visited.

He heard Dr. Charles ask once, "You are giving him a prophylactic antibiotic drip?"

"I don't think that's necessary," the white one replied.

"It's common practice in the hospitals in Europe," Dr. Charles said. He had gone to Paris where his color was no hindrance to his degree. "I guess New Orleans hasn't caught up."

Shortly after, the nurse came with the clear medicine drip and plugged the needle into Leo's arm.

He was asleep when they rolled him away for the cutting and sewing of his muscles that wouldn't cooperate.

Dr. Charles sat next to Leo's mother and father in the waiting room along with others from the neighborhood. The surgery worked and, after a while, with the help of his sisters, Leo began to walk.

In his adolescent years, Leo's mother allowed him to stay outside with the other boys until dark. After their chores and before dinner, they played games and talked about sports personalities and girls' figures. They called him Crip. They called others in the group Scibble Head, Butsy, and Bowl. It wasn't as good as Rock, Runner, or Horse. But he was included.

At that time too, his body began to adapt. His muscles melded as did his nerves. He even began to walk almost smoothly. Not like now, when it took all of his strength to push his body forward.

In the past, the boys in the neighborhood used horseback and bicycles to get around. A few years later, they got access to their father's jalopies. So they ventured farther—out to the colored side of the lake for picnics with girls, near Spanish Fort to look at the waves crash against the debris, over to the riverside to take the ferry to Algiers—distant expeditions—that could now be taken in less than 15 minutes on the interstate.

Sometimes in their early years, the boys went to parties en masse. One night, they walked in a babbling clot to the Saint Peter Claver cafeteria and, after being checked for switchblades, they filtered one-by-one through the door. The handsome boys went through the door first—Booney and Hammer. Then Melvin and Lawrence, the average-looking ones. Then, Leo slipped in with Shy Alfred and Mouse Turd. The band played Ellington and Armstrong. The crowd jitterbugged. Leo watched.

When the Sadie Hawkins song came on, Leo pretended not to notice that no one came by. Then she did, Fat Joyce. She reached out her hand and he took it. They were able to shuffle together in the corner for a long time before anyone admitted they were watching.

Later, a few people teased him, "Crip and Fat Joyce getting married."

His friends didn't comment.

When the boys got older, they sat only a few pews from him in church. In their polyester suits—powder blue, tulip pink and canary yellow—they looked like exotic birds sitting on a wire. They didn't flicker when the priest talked about fidelity and virginity—the same priest who flirted with the neighborhood women when he got drunk. Leo and all of his friends tried their best in church not to roll their eyes and to keep their faith.

Leo was still single, but the same priest had already consecrated the marriages of about half of his friends, several of whose wives were already showing under their off-white, homemade wedding dresses. Later, the priest had baptized their babies—the ones they raised at home with their wives, and also their outside children—the ones with their mistresses.

Leo finally met a priest he actually liked. Father Johns came to Leo's house and took off his collar before he poured himself a water glass full of whiskey. He had been in World War II and knew the difference between real sin and harmless amusements. He was the one who introduced Leo to his wife, a housekeeper at the rectory. Teresita worked there because she had grown up in the orphanage. She was the caramel-colored illegitimate child of a prominent, godless Creole who lived two blocks away but didn't acknowledge her. The priest had become like her older brother.

Soon, Leo and Teresita married. Their early years were their best. Father came over almost every Sunday after mass and Teresita cooked. She made a good table—sometimes a big, pot-roasted pork with sweet potatoes, little peas, gumbo and long-grained rice. Other times, grillades in dark brown tomato gravy over white potatoes and corn-on-the-cob with bread pudding and rum sauce for dessert. Occasionally, she cut open the overripe figs from the yard and sprinkled coarse, sparkling sugar on them.

Leo invited his relatives often. They arrived in all stages of breaking and keeping the Commandments. There were some so sinful that they didn't dare look Father in the eyes, even when he beckoned them over. But others were so innocent and childlike that they sat at the table, smiled, and held his hand.

Teresita and Leo were true to one another, were each other's one and only. They had grown plump and healthy together. Until recently.

He was half-way to his house now from the Circle Food Store. People told him that they would give him a ride, but he preferred to walk. Then, he had a little time to remember.

Teresita had gotten sick first. The new doctor said it was her heart. But he didn't really care enough to find out if there was anything more. Every old person has heart trouble, Leo thought. And by the look in the doctor's eyes—the glazed expression when he faced them on the other side of the desk and the glances to his watch and phone—Leo knew that Teresita was not going to get any more of the doctor's attention.

In her weakened state, Teresita took to the bed. Leo became flooded with memories of what it meant to be crippled and sick, and the feeling of seeing the sunrise thankful that you hadn't gone in the night. Every morning, he sat in a chair next to his wife's bed while she slept. He stayed until his stomach rumbled, and he had to get up to fix breakfast.

Lately, she didn't want to eat the scrambled eggs and grits that he cooked.

Now, he headed back to the house with different groceries. It was a long painful walk, but he rolled a red metal cart full of paper bags. He didn't want to press his luck. His back was beginning to deteriorate. The doctors said they would not do another surgery at his age.

He walked up to the house. It was built by his friends—all of them were in the trades in one way or another—carpenters, contractors, painters. Some of them were also musicians. But that kind of work never paid. He had hired the musicians and the fulltime workmen to build the house for Teresita and him. He was employed as a bookkeeper. He had taught himself, and he could sit in a chair and work numbers for a long time. His friends had dropped out of school because they said they needed to be active.

The living room and dining room were just like Teresita wanted it—big enough to invite the neighborhood. They came too. Loutie, Melvin Sr., Thomas, and crazy Chapon. Even the white girl next door breeched their steps a few weeks earlier. But she didn't stay, she just wanted to show Teresita the way to cook figs into a biscuit, as if she hadn't learned to cook more than 50 years ago. She even knew the best way to garden and to feed nature by letting the yard go fallow every few seasons so that the bees could thrive.

Leo sometimes wrote notes on college ruled paper to his relatives who moved away. He asked them to return home for a visit. Often the letters came back with familiar print on the envelope saying addressee unknown. A few of his relatives had run away from New Orleans, thinking that people in other places would be perfect.

Leo knew better. He once was crippled, and now he was whole, even though he could hardly walk straight. Everyone was a cripple in some way at one time or another.

He pulled the grocery cart up the front steps. It was a last effort in a long walk that always took too much energy. He opened the glass-paned door to his house.

The front room smelled beautiful—brown gravy and onions. The aroma of coffee from this morning still wafted in the corners of the room. Teresita must have felt better, momentarily, maybe just this evening, enough for them to sit and eat together.

Maybe for the last time. It was always the last time until it wasn't.

He walked into the front room and pushed the grocery cart aside. There was nothing in it so precious that it would spoil. He called Teresita from the kitchen and clicked on the radio to their favorite station.

He put his arms almost around her girth and held her tight. He put his face close to her tight curls and smelled the salt and coconut oil in her scalp. He nuzzled her thick soft hair. Then, they danced slowly, hardly moving their feet for as long as they could.

Lost and Found

What Went Missing

The Hotels

"**G**et up, old man. Somebody got to earn a living." Sweet Pea wakes me every morning with a laugh. I just look at her.

She's got scrawny, white eyebrows going every which away that use to be thick, black and tamed. She's got a face that sags on the underside that is full of odd, little hairs and brown bumps. That skin, I used to feel it so smooth under my hand. I would take her pointy chin between my thumb and first finger, and hold her, and give her a tiny squeeze and a shake before I'd kiss her, sometimes on the cheek, sometimes on the lips.

Now those lips are sloppy too, flat and mush mouth. She drips when she leans over the bed and calls my name, "Davis." She flaps those loose lips over my head, and I realize that I have just fallen asleep again.

"That hotel ain't going to wait for you to open, you know," she tells me. "Breakfast on the table."

I get up and look at myself in the mirror. I'm a little shorter than I used to be, especially in the evening. My pajamas sag in the seat when I am wearing them. Unless she takes them out for me, I go to sleep just in my boxers.

"Big drawers," she calls them. "Big drawers" as opposed to little drawers that we see in the newspaper on the fancy men they have now, and we laugh.

I am wearing pajamas this morning, bottom and top, and so I can go to the table without putting on a robe. She already got a spread on: grits and toast, eggs and bacon, dark coffee, thick from her waking up this morning and having it drip for two hours now. It's 7 a.m., and I'm going to work even if they say there's going to be a storm. This is the third time this summer they said it.

My Sweet Pea is making my plate, and it's on the table by the time I sit. She kisses the top of my head, and I smack her on the rump.

"You a good mare," I tell her, and she knows it's true. We been on this ranch a long time, this mare and me, her mule. It's our joke that a mare is a pretty horse, and all a mule does is work.

The Ninth Ward still looks like the farm to us. We got a little land around the house. We grow some tomatoes in the back yard. We got yams running out there in the fall. We even might get ourselves a few watermelon. Melons are real sweet on this soft land. It is good for small farming, and that was our intention when we moved closer to New Orleans. Just a little farm on the edge of town, an acre or two, and then maybe some children.

We had them, and then, so fast, the children all up and went. But when the children was here, the farm got parceled off. We needed more money and each time somebody came to offer us cash for a little land. We said "Why not, a bird in the hand is good, yes?"

Since then, we got some good neighbors out of the bargain. Miss Otis with them two boys and two girls. Mr. Brown with that girl who play piano. We got Mrs. Jewel, Mrs. Dana, and Jacks. Houses is all around us now. We farmed up people not plants. Anyway, people are better.

The last time the hotel call me in for regular work was six month ago. Then they need some men. I ain't used to getting up every day, but the social security don't give us much. So when I can make a few dollars, I go in. The hotel glad to see somebody know what they doing.

Sweet Pea send me off with a paper bag. "Take this here with you in case you get hungry." She know I don't get much hungry no more. I used to have a young man's appetite 30, must have been 40 years ago, when I was in my prime. That's when I gave Sweet Pea the hardest life. And she stuck by me even then.

I was having women all back of Canal Street. They comed in for the holidays, Mardi Gras, Sugar Bowl. They stay up in the other hotels, and they dying for a black man. Then I thought, who was I to let them go away without some satisfaction. I regret it now. Sweet Pea getting whiff of them on my clothes. But more, me talking to her like that. Like if she was crazy. That's all a weak man got, just a excuse on somebody else.

"You crazy, Sweet Pea. You need to get yourself something better to do than come after me like that," I used to tell her that, knowing full well I was guilty.

She knowed it too, but she let me go. I don't know why. But she did.

The kids were small then. The last three were in the house. I could see her turning to them, cooking them something, or taking them somewhere away.

"Come on, y'all," she said to them. "They ain't nothing here in this house for people. Let's go outside. See what I got growing." She'd take them in the yard, and in a few minutes they would be spraying the hose and laughing.

And I remember standing up to the screen door, too scared to make a move for wondering if I was going to start us up to fighting again. But feeling so much like I wanted to join them.

They growed up and gone now. Now I wonder if I shouldn't have join them then because now I can't.

Me and Sweet Pea stop talking for a long time after that. Must have been years. When the kids got to teenagers and was off to the football games and out on their dates, Sweet Pea join the church. She and Miss Otis would bake together and go out maybe three, four nights a week. I was working a lot.

Doing a hotel is good work, when you can find the right spot. If you don't have no bad boss, some white boy who think just cause he got out of UNO he could tell you what to do. Some of them come on like that but they don't last. They run away to Metairie or to Baton Rouge, get in some business where they don't have to run into people, get them a truck, make babies. They happy.

Sometimes you lucky enough to have one who know what he don't know. Then they leave you alone unless you ask for them. That's a kind of boss I had for a long while.

"Get yourself out now," Sweet Pea is calling me from the bedroom. So I got to get dressed and catch the bus.

"Good morning," the bus driver tell me when I pull up to the third step. He's nice enough to make everybody calm and wait. I move a little slower these days. Some of them bus drivers want to press on the air brakes and pump while they waiting for you to get on. Make you feel older than ever, or either you mad that they don't have no manners. This one is just fine.

"All right now," I say hello when I get on and take a seat about mid-way down the aisle. Save the front seats for the old women. They'll get on when we pass near Rampart and the Iberville projects. They got cleaning jobs up and down Canal Street. But hardly nobody on the bus this morning.

Katrina's out in the Gulf.

Before Katrina, there was Cindy. Every time I stay home with Sweet Pea and we wait, even days, before figuring out whether

146

we going ride it out. We watching television. We listening to the radio. They scare the people so bad. The weatherman come on and tell you all about how there was Betsy and then Camille, and how Canal Street going to look like a lake with the water up to the hotels' second floors. How we got to get out of the city, because from Grand Isle on up to St. Bernard going to turn back to sea water.

Me and Sweet Pea, we got scared last time. We take all of our stuff into the car. Took us a whole day to pack everything. Put water and a ice chest full of Diet Pepsi and beer. Got us bread and sandwich food so we could stop in a hotel somewhere north of Baton Rouge. I went get gas, took a hour in the line. We get on Highway 90 because Sweet Pea don't like the interstate. And what happen? We sit.

All the time, Sweet Pea turning one station to the other. She flipping the radio back and forth so much I get mad.

"For God sake, ain't you satisfied that they all saying the same thing?" I holler at her. Then I'm ashamed of myself. "I'm sorry," I said.

That's what I learned by now. All it take is some being sorry to make her happy. Funny how all the time I was young, I was so sorry, and I didn't know it, and I sure couldn't say it.

Sorry is when you know you made a mistake, and even before you really know it sometimes, just you got a feeling that you put something out of whack. And you know it was you. That's sorry, and you just got to say it.

How come women know that already, I will never understand. But they do. And it took this man many years to find that out. That's something about life, if you're lucky, you learn. If you lucky enough to get old.

That day we evacuated for Cindy, Sweet Pea and me went against all of our natural feelings. The weather wasn't that bad, just kind of breezy and dark, but there wasn't no smell in the air of the salt that you get when a real storm is coming. It wasn't cool and still with no birds, or quiet so when your voice came out so clear it was like you were talking inside your empty coffee cup.

Difference is, when it's the day before a real hurricane, the sky is about as clear as you've ever seen. It's the most beautiful day made by God. You think can't hurricanes exist at all in this world. Then, it happen.

You could be standing on your porch and the wind build. It get rainy all of a sudden, almost like the summer storms, but less fickle. It's like this rain knows it's getting bigger. So for the first 15 minutes you think "Well, this a pretty strong rain." Then it don't let up. It get stronger raining, and stronger. Then the wind start to blow along with that, and your plants in the pots start easing across your porch, if you ain't took them in then. Now, you know you better. And you better go catch your garbage can and your tools too, if you ain't had everything tied down. Because you realize that everything ain't tied down going to fly. And then you begin wondering if somebody else's stuff ain't tied down and going to come flying into your house. You scared your windows going to break and your place be a screaming mess. About then you call on God.

Me and Sweet Pea, we never board the windows. We tape them, just in case something break the window. If you got boards on your house and you got to get out in a hurry, you can't do that. And if the glass break, we figure we get new furniture anyway. What's a little water from a little broken glass? If it's too much water, then all of the Ninth Ward be gone. All of New Orleans gone. Then what's the use?

Like this morning when I ride the bus, I could see folk from all over who made their homes here in the Ninth Ward. They got the country people—people from out of the Parishes who come upriver. They left their pirogues and shacks to be where they could get work, but they didn't want to live in the city. When I ride the bus a little further up I see the people in the old houses around Franklin

Avenue. They had them a little money once but not much. They shotguns is wide and the wood is turned nice on the cornices, but now ain't nobody paint them. Then through the Seventh Ward, I remember all the parades for the Creole Fiesta, the Corpus Christi School fair. That float that my club member's son was on in first grade. All the people who came to be doctors, politicians and teachers, they lived in the Seventh Ward once. But now they gone. Most of they mommas and daddies are dead.

And at the projects and Dooky's where the bus turn, I used to wait for the Zulu. Don't have that much energy no more. Plus they shooting. Lord.

But this morning, everybody starting to hat up for Katrina. I told Sweet Pea I'd call her if it really seem like it's going to be bad, and she could join me at the hotel. That's the best place anyway in a hurricane. The floors are high. The things are built of steel. That's why she tell me, "Go to work. Make some money. I got to buy me a red dress."

She a good woman.

That last time, when she and me get in the car and go evacuate like they telling us on television and the radio, we just get stuck on Highway 90. We even try get on the interstate since everything going so slow.

And what you know, the interstate creeping. We sit in the car for six hours, pull off the road twice for gas. We eat and drink everything in the ice chest. And the weather still don't look bad. So I tell her, "Sweet Pea, you know what I'm going to do."

She say, "I'm with you Daddy."

So we go back home.

The traffic is not so bad going in reverse. We some of the few people going back to the Ninth Ward. All the time, the man on the radio practically screaming now about how the water going to come up high, how the wind going be so bad, how the people better get on the road now or watch out. The storm never came.

Sweet Pea and me, we look at each other, and she say it first, "Never again." We laughing together because we know it's the truth.

The hotel I'm working at is one of these new, all glass ones. They put it up a few years ago like you can't believe. Machines that swing the steel up over your head, maybe 10 floors. Then, things to help catch the steel that they bring up and then the glass. You would think glass would be falling out on to the ground all the time, shattering out on the sidewalk for a block wide. But nothing fall. It goes up there so neat that when they finish construction, it is like they put together a jigsaw puzzle. Everything fits together so tight and nice.

Me and Sweet Pea, we are now a perfect couple. That's what everybody says when they meet her. It's a wonder to me now how that could have happened.

The one thing I did was figured I wanted the fighting to be over, and I wanted somebody as nice as Sweet Pea to like me, even though I probably didn't deserve it. It came one day like a real need. I was sitting in that French Quarter bar, white women on each side. They laughing and laughing because something I said sounded so "amusing." And then I begin to think, I ain't that interesting.

So I began to act like just me. I stopped smiling. I drank my beer and ordered another one. I started to look at the horse races on the television, and when them women started talking to me, I said, "Now shush a moment. The horses is at the gate." And what they do. They laugh like that's the funniest thing in the world. I had to get out of there.

I began to act like Sweet Pea had told me to all the time. I began working more and bringing my money to her, rather than spending it all out in the street. I began treating her like I would other women. Being polite to her, even giving her a compliment some times.

Maybe some men knowed to do that all along. I used to see them when I was still hitting the pavement. When I'm coming home, they going to church with their wives and children. Or at the hotel, they waiting outside the room while she finished getting her stuff. They'd sometimes be watching the kids and holding her purse while they waited in the hotel hallways. "Punks," I used to say to myself.

Somebody look at me now might say, "punk." But more likely they say, "old ass punk."

You know what though, I think other men had many more years of happiness in life than I did. Funny, how wildness ain't enough.

"Yes sir." I get to my job near the bell captain. Long as I'm there on time and doing my job, I don't have to socialize with anyone. I like to keep my thoughts to myself. And seem like I'm thinking all of the time lately of things that came before. But it take longer sometimes to make the thought into a word, so it's a good thing nobody ask me, "What you thinking?" They just happy to get they bags picked up and taken out to the taxicabs.

Lots of people seem to be getting up.

They all in a panic this morning because they say that Katrina is going to be a category 5, bigger than Betsy. Betsy wasn't nothing to sniff at. Me and Sweet Pea, we went to her mother's house in the Seventh Ward that time. Even then it was kind of scary. We took the kids with us and we brought the food. I was drinking the hard stuff then, and me and her father, we just sat in the back drinking while the storm was coming on.

We could hear the garbage cans all around us rattling down the street when the wind got up. That was the first noisy thing we heard. The next was the wind howling like an animal. At first, we wondered if it was some old dog in the neighborhood whose voice we never recognized because it didn't really holler much. It was like a funny kind of hound that went, "Oue- oue- oue." Then Sweet Pea's momma said, "It's the wind." That send a shudder through all of us. It about sobered me up. I don't know about Sweet Pea's father. He like to booze no matter what the occasion.

But Sweet Pea herself, she look at me, with a real look, not the kind she had been having all those years when I was fooling around. In those years, her eyes would say, "OK fool, I know you are lying, and I just about hate you." It was a hard look that made me wonder whether we would ever be able to understand each other again.

But that night, the night of the hurricane Betsy, Sweet Pea look at me like, "I have knowed you for a long time, and you are a friend of mine." And I felt that if I died that night, there would have been something in my life that was all right.

We heard the shingles hitting the ground off the roof. They were sharp little pings that stood out in the howling wind. We saw some leaks start then too in the corners of the ceiling, and for a while, we wondered if the whole ceiling was going to come down around our ears.

But Sweet Pea's dad was one of those country carpenters, and he kept explaining to all of us how he himself had made that ceiling so that it was strong cross beams and wire and plaster. And maybe we were in some trouble if the plaster got wet. But it was going to take a lot of water to make that plaster come down. He had set it in the driest days of October and watched it dry himself.

Sweet Pea had the kids sit around a candle and say some prayers before she told them it was time for bed. She let them fall asleep wrapped in sheets on the floor near us. We all slept together in the same room that night. I stayed awake as long as I could, and I woke up with Sweet Pea's daddy tapping me on the shoulder and calling me with his finger to come outside and see. I crept out of the house, just him and me, at about dawn to see what the hurricane have done.

The 30-foot cherry tree in the backyard had been uprooted. There were pecans all over the ground blown in from the trees on the other street. I thought I'd send the kids out there to pick them up.

There were patches of roofs off in many of them houses. And the tin shed next door was leaning so that the walls and part of the roof touched the ground. I could see far away that the tops of trees on a nearby street were in a tangle, leaning in all different directions.

Sweet Pea's daddy's house wasn't bad though. The tiles we heard were lying on the sidewalk. And other than that and some branches in the yard, he was all right.

Of course, wasn't no electricity and water for a couple days. But it reminded me of my days in the country. I told that to my children. Sweet Pea gave me the Amen.

"Y'all just too soft," I told them.

"Get yourselves outside and pick up them pecans. I could make some good pie with that," Sweet Pea told them, and they cheered up and went on.

It was only when we decided to try going home the next day that we saw the real damage from the hurricane.

The water had rose when the levee broke. People said it was the city's doing.

"I tell you my cousin heard them put the dynamite to the levee," Miss Otis said. We saw her in the street when she came look at her house.

"Ain't no rest for the weary," she said. "It's a conspiracy."

I never did think somebody blew up the levee to flood us out, although the flood of the Ninth Ward did keep the water from backing up over the white folks. But I don't believe even white people would go send somebody out to ruin the lives of so many of us. They believe in Hell too.

But inside the hotel now, you could see, it take all kind. They, most of them, racing around to get out. I'm bringing their bags to taxis. They sharing cars now. There are some people who tip a lot, feeling sorry for me. There are those who just won't see me at all, probably for the same reason. And there are others who talk to me like they knowed me their whole lives, and for some reason once we get to talking, it's like I knowed them. It's funny, but that's how it is.

That day Sweet Pea and me turned back in the car from hurricane Cindy, we said to each other, although not in so many words—we survived Betsy so this can't be nothing.

It's all in the Lord's hands anyway. We tried to evacuate Cindy. We couldn't get out. Today the man call me to work. This is the plan that the Lord got for us. We following it. The only thing I regret now, is that Sweet Pea didn't come with me.

When I call her up on the phone, she tells me that she is making lunch and that the television is still now saying Category 3, down from 5.

"What you think? I ought to catch the bus come by you?" Sweet Pea asks.

"Why don't you start packing?" I tell her. "Seem like I could find somebody here come and pick you up."

We say "All right," "Goodbye."

The tourists are flying out of this hotel, suitcases after suitcases. I am going back and forth to the curb. I never notice when darkness begins to fall and the shift ahead of me has left. Anybody I know with a car is gone. "I'm on my way home now," I call to tell Sweet Pea. But the phone rings and rings. She don't answer.

If you ever rode the bus downtown, you know isn't one of them that come less than every 20 minutes. Add to that a hurricane is coming, and so many bus drivers never showed up for work, and you will expect to wait at the stop for an hour or more.

What do people do when they waiting for the bus? When the weather is sunny, you'll see them shifting from place to place around the bus stop. They are trying to follow the shade. They try to stay cool with a wet handkerchief back of their necks. They will take the handkerchief out of their pocket or purse where they all have it, and then they will take the bottle of water that they refilled from home, and they will wet the handkerchief. Don't think that they would wring it out. The weather is too hot for that, and they know that the sun will dry up the handkerchief. So they put it sopping on the back of their necks. The top of their shirt collars get wet. The water runs down to their underwear, sopping their bras and undershirts at the place where the run off catch. But for a moment they are cool even in the midday sun.

When waiting for the bus on a cloudy day, there is nothing else to do but think.

The people wonder whether the young men who pass in a car are checking them out as a robbery victim, or whether anyone they know will pass, ask them if they want to get picked up. Or if somebody will be on the bus to have a conversation. They think about the conversation they will have on the bus, whether they need to tell people that their little cousin is pregnant or if folks already know, and they'll think not saying anything is a front. They think maybe they'll talk about their bosses so they really don't have to say anything.

Me, I'm at the hotel, wondering whether Sweet Pea made it out to the bus on time or whether the buses were being taken out of service. Finally, I made it to a phone. The RTA said that many of the routes had been suspended because of the coming storm. My route was one of them.

There were a very few new people arriving, mostly from the other hotels that were putting them out. Everybody's going crazy, I thought, when do a hotel not want guests?

I went back and stood with the bell captain. And soon I was alone. Somebody came and picked him up. I waited and wondered. Then I called Sweet Pea again. Nothing.

It was getting dark when Sweet Pea called at the desk. "Old man," she said, "You are really something."

"I been trying to call you. Where you been?" I tried not to raise my voice. But I heard myself coming out loud.

I heard her hesitate. She was trying to be patient with me, and I was sorry again. Always sorry. But I didn't apologize this time. There was no place for it.

"Look, where you at? Why you not here?" I asked her.

"The bus pick me up, and then brought me about half way and then went out of service," she said. "I walked back home."

I could imagine her walking on the summer streets. New Orleans was getting so mean. An old lady with a big pocketbook full of water bottles and photographs, because she always carries the pictures of our children when she evacuates. I saw her walking down Galvez and then over the Industrial Canal bridge without even a soul asking her, "Mother, where you going?"

"Why didn't you get a ride?"

"What you think I'm going to stick my thumb out like some kind of hippie?"

"At least you home now," I told her. "I'll see if I can't get somebody to pick you up."

"What? So we could sit on the highway again? I rather ride it out. It's not so bad out there anyway."

"I don't know about that," I told her. There was no sense in arguing now.

There was nobody that wanted to get out in that wind and the blowing rain to go get Sweet Pea. So I went into the garage. I hadn't did this since I was young, and I had to find an old car. All these new ones have those electronic things.

So I went over to a nice car that was old and simple, and American made so I could understand the wiring. It was parked in the back next to the view over the river. For some reason, it was still warm. I opened the heavy hood, bent into the engine, and tied together the wire. I was faster when I was younger, but I could still do it. Then I got in the car, and I was gone.

Life is like a ride in a stolen car. You hot and rushed when you're young like you're getting away from something. Then for a while you are speeding down the road, just noticing that you're doing it alone. You driving fast, and not paying attention to anybody else. All around you there are people in cars and even people in your car. But you don't see them. Until, when you start to get tired of what you're doing. You been driving so long, you start to notice the people and things you're passing. Just when you start to enjoy the ride, you're there, at your final destination.

That's the way my ride to get Sweet Pea felt. I raced out of the French Quarter, took Charters Street, across Esplanade to the Elysian Fields. I got out of the hotel district so fast so nobody would notice me. Then I began to think about what I was doing.

First, I'd put her in the car. Then we'd come back up to Canal Street. That was about the safest place by this time. If the storm was going to hit, there was about nowhere safe. If the wind didn't get us, the water would. Maybe if we went inside the ballroom in the center of the hotel, then we could be safe from the wind that would most likely destroy all the glass. But at least we'd be up above the flooding.

As I drove and I ain't drove for a long time, I saw the streets of New Orleans in a different way. Most of the time, they were full of people, and that made them different because now they looked shabby and grey.

Gusts of wind blowed the dust from the front yards away from abandoned tricycles and garbage into the path of the car. The streets were covered already with debris and big cracks were already in the pavement. This was not from the storm, but of the city never really giving a damn.

157

But it never looked as bad to me as today when I bumped over the trash and down into the cracks. The car bounced on bad shocks. My hands sweat. The wind shifted the car from lane to lane.

Especially when I got on the top of the Industrial Canal Bridge, I could see the water choppy and frightening even from the corner of my eye. How come I never really thought of it as dangerous, only wide and beautiful, something to be proud of?

The life of the water and the boats swaying and rocking now seemed bigger than all the small houses butted up to the dry side of the canal. My Sweet Pea was in one of them.

I stepped on the gas, and the car tires spun a few times before catching on the bridge grate and jerking into motion.

Even with the wind banging the back screen door and the shutters on the windows, Sweet Pea was asleep when I got there.

"Man, I am too tired from all that walking," she told me, and she only opened her eyes slightly.

"Come get in the car," I told her.

"Can't man. Too tired," she whispered. Her breathing was slow, and when I tried to pick her up, I felt like my back was going to break.

I went outside looking for Miss Otis or Jacks, or any of the boys. Nobody's cars were around. People's houses were closed.

I went back and looked at my baby. She had on her best dress. It was a thin thing where you could see the slip through it. Her shoes were still on her feet. Her arm was over her head on the pillow. She was so tired. I tried to pick her up again. Dead weight. I went to turn on the television, but the electricity was already gone.

I was panting and could hardly breathe when I came to the side of the bed. I got in with her. I stroked her white hair, put my arms around her waist, and spooned my body around hers. I felt peace as the house shook all around us and the streetlights went dark.

II.

We had my mama packed to go to Baton Rouge. But she wouldn't leave with my cousin if I wasn't going, and I had to work. So after the boss let us off at the restaurant, I got in the car, picked up her, my girl and the baby, and we were on our way to the hotel.

It cost a lot, but why else do I work until two in the morning? To say "yes sir" to tourists who smile at me when I'm handing them a plate, but who would call the cops if I walked too close behind them on the street? To be called stupid by bosses who never went to college? To walk through the neighborhood looking totally lame in a cheap white shirt and thin black pants?

I work to bring groceries home, to pay the rent, to get clothes for my girl and the baby. And once in a while we get a treat, like tonight, we stay at the hotel.

When the wind is high, we'll be up on one of the safe floors. Mama was in Betsy so she gets skittish when the hurricanes come around. We left for Cindy, all the way to Baton Rouge, and the day of the hurricane was about as beautiful as they come. This time, the weatherman's saying Category 5. So we're not going to play.

The baby is dressed pretty when I pick them up and my girl smells nice. Not like someone who is evacuating. Her hair is slicked back with curls to the side that I know she took time on. My mama is carrying plates of food in brown paper bags.

"We don't want to buy no expensive hotel food," she says.

I laugh. She's right, of course. The food will be too much money and not as good as home. But I tell her anyway, "I got this. We could eat at the restaurant all you want." So she don't feel worried.

Once everybody's in the car, I slam the doors hard. This old car is American-made so it takes slamming to close everything, and then it's like we're in a tank. I got it on sale from one of my neighbors down the street. He gets a new car every few years. But this is the car he saved for his kids and then got a new one for his kids then sold it to me. The price was right, and I can run to work and back. That's all I needed.

When I get home in the morning, my girl has breakfast fixed. Mama used to make it but she's getting older. She used to be up before the sun came out. She had coffee boiling, bacon fried, and eggs waiting to be cracked and scrambled.

"You work hard, you eat well," she always said. So now, even though she can't do that for me, my girl does.

She raised her brothers and sisters. She made the breakfasts, did the hair, ironed the clothes—and later showed the little ones how to press their uniforms. Her mama and daddy worked. That's how they all went to college. All of them except her went. She keep saying that she's going to Delgado for her nursing degree, and I say, "Go on." But now that the baby's here, she says, "Wait until he get a little older."

She's just good like that. Everybody else first.

She taught me something. I used to run the street in high school, go round with Who Shot John. My mama tried to tell me to watch the company I was keeping. And a lot of girls wanted me to like them by making me jealous. I'd go out. Then, I'd see them out. They'd be flirting with other people. So would I. That ended it. Too many times.

Andra, here, she said, "If you want me, you be here." And she meant it. She stayed home and I stayed home. She sealed the deal. And since then I can see why she acted like that. It's the way everything works. She doesn't need any "lost souls." That's what she calls the brothers who can't get it together with their women, their jobs, or their homes. Andra has the house, the baby, even Mama in order. She takes care of my food and clothes, and last herself.

If she was ever on a sinking ship, she'd be the one to go down with it. I'd be standing right next to her.

The car clunks its way up the indoor parking lot. We find a space near the edge on the 10th floor. New Orleans is a beautiful sight from the garage. I can see the small brick buildings of the French Quarter, the warehouses, Algiers, the river's crescent. I have to say I love this place.

We get our suitcases and paper bags from the car and we go down in the elevator. The lobby is filled with people going the other way. I hear they trying to get cabs (which people tell them to share), rental cars (ain't no more), and planes (they wish). Obvious, some never been in a hurricane.

Right now, they in one of the safest places in town. They high above the water if it flood and, by being in the Quarter, they on the highest land. The men are shouting for service. Some of them white women look ready to cry. Mama tells one, "Ain't nothing to worry about, Miss." But she looks at Mama like she's speaking another language. Her friend, though, got the good manners to say, "Thank you."

We wait our turn and get to the counter. "We need a room for tonight," I say. But before I can get it out of my mouth good, the man at the desk say, "I'm sorry. We're booked."

"Ain't people coming out of here?" Andra taps me on the shoulder and whisper.

"Ain't people leaving right now?" I ask the man.

He looks us up and down. Then, directly in the face, he say to me, "If we have rooms, which we don't, we're not renting them."

I seen that look before. It means, "Not to you, nigger." And I know how to respond with my fists.

But my people are standing behind me. Andra's leaning over my shoulder. And I know Mama's getting tired holding that plate wrapped up in the brown paper bag. So I turn to her first, take the plate, then I say to the fellow at the desk, "Man, it's a hurricane coming."

"I believe I know that," he says, and he calls the next person in line.

So here are my choices. I could call this man out with the names that come to mind. I could get loud and, as Mama says, "Act my color." But I figure this is 2005, and I am the man of this family. So I tell everybody, "Y'all, step back." I take a breath, and I think of another plan. The first one would land us all in Parish Prison. Don't want to go there again.

The first time, I was not even speeding home from work. The cops picked me up, said they were looking for someone who committed a crime, and I fit that description. Black is all they meant. And young. Isn't a person like me in New Orleans that doesn't fit the description, and not just in New Orleans. Black men getting arrested and shot all over America. I kept my cool that night, went along, but they still put me in lockup.

I never got a phone call until the morning. Andra was so worried that she answered on the first ring. "Lord, where you?" she asked. And when I told her, she never said, "What did you do?" She said, "How much you need?" She got $500 from our friends by that afternoon. It was almost worth being in jail to see her move into action like that.

I say almost because being in jail is never really worth it. Central lockup was full of noise and sickness. Men spitting and coughing. Men pissing right out in public. Some of them wanted other people to see. Sick-in-they-mind men. Sad men, peoples' daddies that was drunk. Even a few who was glad to be off the street. You could see that all the noise and confusion made them feel safe. They were so quiet.

Never ever never ever never again do I want that to happen to me. This is the reason, I told everybody to step back and to breathe.

I ask Mama if she wanted to go back home. We on the Esplanade Ridge anyway. So we shouldn't flood. We could go to

McDonough 42 if the water come. But she shake her head no. I shouldn't even have ask. I know she's afraid. I didn't need to make her admit it. So we go to what they call on the radio, the shelter of last resort. I leave my car in the parking lot where I know it will be dry.

We catch a bus to the Superdome. We just got in when the wind was starting to kick up.

III.

M y new husband is the most beautiful man. His eyelashes are black and long. They curl softly upward against his cheeks when he sleeps. His dark hair makes rings around the edges of his ears. His jaw is square, and there is a bit of stubble around the edge of his face, but not too much. He hardly needs to shave.

I pass my hand over his bare neck, his shoulders, down his back and his hips just to feel their muscles, and the way that they curve. He hardly moves.

"Go back to sleep," I tell him. I touch him again along his legs. His body is mine now. I want him to see me and want me, to respond to my ache.

But I don't want to wake him and tell him about the hurricane. That would cut our honeymoon short. I want to spend each moment that I can with him like this.

Yesterday, we got married at this hotel. My whole family was there. My cousin was my maid-of-honor, and she wore a beautiful pink dress that her sister sewed. My father came in from Buras.

I know that they hated to lose me to New Orleans.

When I left home, it was as if I was going away for the rest of my life. My relatives lined up on the dock where they keep the family boat next to the house. I got in the car on the road, up high. They all looked like children, some of them holding hands, the others standing knock-kneed and waiting. When I waved, they all waved in unison.

No nursing schools are out in the country, and somebody needed to work. But all they ever heard about New Orleans made them act like I was going to school to become a prostitute.

"Won't you stay here and get you a good, country man?" one cousin asked.

"Ain't they a lot of niggers in New Orleans?" asked another.

I couldn't tell them that I had always felt that I was going away, and I was not afraid of anyone.

I stayed a good girl. I couldn't tell them that I slept with no one the whole time I was at Delgado College, and the time I was taking my practicals at Charity. There were men who came on to me, plenty of guys my age and my race. But they didn't offer me anything.

It's like if you've eaten catfish all of your life. You really don't want any more catfish.

College just confirmed that.

I met men with the girls from my classes. There were others from country towns. They had left all their people too. We got together on the weekends.

We went to places to drink. Beer, and after beer, laughing, at what I can't remember now. Boys approaching us, and us turning them away, or I should say, I was.

Ellen, the girl from St. Charles, she had them coming in and out of her room all the time. Every weekend there was another boy. "I like to see the difference," she said. And she related for us in medical and not so medical terms, what made a good lover.

"It ain't about size," she said, "It's about specialty."

"It's a medical joke," I repeated it to a guy one night. I was trying to be funny. But he didn't laugh. The person who was there at that bar really wasn't me.

I was the person who waved goodbye with a broken heart to family who wanted more for me, but couldn't give it.

Nurses fix things. That's all I knew from the beginning. I told my high school counselor. She replied, "They ain't no schools down here like that."

I could have taken Agriculture, English, Education and so many other things to keep me near my home town. But I still wouldn't have been satisfied.

After my mother left, everyone believed that I was following in her footsteps. For them, she was just a woman who came into town, married a good local man, then ran away, breaking his heart.

"Just like the mother." I didn't have to hear them to know that's what went around. My mother had more ambition, and it was in my genes, I guess. It's a shame that I never heard where she went.

If my father knew, he never told me. And the good Lord knows, I asked. From the time I was a little girl to just before now when I was making out the wedding invitations.

"If I knewed where she went, I never would of held it back," my father said.

"Life is a hurting thing," he told me when I was little.

The sadness was always on his face. Our evening house was quiet with him always reading the bills. I tried to dance in front of him, tell him jokes, sing the songs I learned in school. That night after a performance, I asked him, "Why don't you clap, Daddy?"

It didn't have nothing to do with me, he said. It was just the pain of being on earth.   .

The wind is whipping around the windows in the sitting room of our hotel suite. We are nestled in the bedroom, and my beautiful husband is still snoring. It's funny how love-making affects men. They can stay up all night drinking and laughing with their friends, and the next day they're clear-headed and ready to go to work. But make love with them for a few hours, and then they are good for nothing.

I excuse him for being a man. I get up and start to pack. I'm sure the hotel will call us any minute to find out our plans. Today we were going to sightsee—as if we knew nothing about New Orleans before now. Tonight we were going to eat in the fancy restaurants.

My family stayed just for the afternoon. They came together and walked through the hotel in a clump. They whispered to one another when they saw a man wearing loafers or a woman in a sari. When they saw all the black people on Canal Street, the girls kind of cowered over their purses, and the men put on their cowboy walks. If it wasn't so embarrassing, I would have laughed.

When I touched the hand of a young black man in the fast food restaurant, I could hear an audible gasp from my cousin May. As if she hadn't been around black people all of her life. She just never touched them. She thought of them only as her personal few—Miss Mable from the vegetable stand, Mrs. Orice's son Luther, and Darnell's sister, Emily. She only thought about them as the people she knew. But in New Orleans, for some reason, as a group, blacks were frightening.

Before I married Bill, when I brought him home, for the first few hours, they couldn't even tell. He has beautiful dark hair. His skin is a kind of yellow tan. He looks like some Cajun boys, but he is from New Orleans so that makes him black. His family is very political.

But he isn't.

That's where we agree. We are individuals. Our lives are not about politics at all. We love each other. If our families don't like that we're different races, that's their problems.

His mother was not too happy. I could tell by the way she asked me, "What does your father do?"

I said, "Mostly fish, M'am." I saw her head drop.

We were at this big ball and so many people like Bill were there too—dark and light people—all of them black—all dressed in evening gowns and tuxedos. I saw his mother move over to one of the older women and whisper something behind her hand. Then they both shook their heads from side-to-side.

I guess they were talking about me. It's not easy being white. Everybody knows Bill is black in New Orleans. They seem to have a secret signal. The light-skinned ones see each other on the street, and they nod, or either they come up and slap one another on the back, and they hug. Seems like we can't go anywhere without Bill having two or three cousins in the vicinity.

The females, they give me a sideways look, as if just because I am there doesn't mean that they have to like me. Then they go on and talk with Bill as if I am deaf. "What does she want to do next week?" they'll ask him about some appointment right in my presence. Most of the time, I just pretend I don't hear. But one time, I told his cousin, a girl about my age, "She likes it if you talk to her instead of being so rude."

Bill's anger was almost worth the look on her face.

"She said she was sorry. She didn't intend to be mean," I told Bill later.

"She wasn't apologizing. She was insulting you more. You just didn't know it," he said. "I wish you would just trust that I can handle my own people."

But then, I couldn't see how he was going to get them to understand that we had a relationship. And that our relationship was bigger than them. They had his past, but his future was with me. I knew it then. He had everything I wanted.

I didn't go out looking for a colored boy. They were just nicer. They talked more softly. They were more polite. They didn't even get as drunk. Not in my presence anyway.

"They just want to get in your pants," May told me. "They think you think they are gorillas anyhow. So they putting on the best of their manners. You think I ain't tried one?" May did bring a black man into the apartment once. He slept with her one time, then he was gone.

But I really didn't see the difference between him and the others who went through her revolving door. A person either sleeps for love or doesn't.

There is no in between.

Bill tried to get in my pants too when we first met, the very first night. He was on fire when he found out my secret.

"You're still a virgin?"

But then, he treated me all the more special. He backed off completely about sleeping with me. He stopped taking me out on dates, true, and I saw him with other girls around campus. But so many nights after he dropped them off, he came by my place to talk. We stayed up hour after hour laughing and talking.

Mostly we talked about family. How mine was old-fashioned and so was his, and how we wanted something different in the future. "You can make it come true," he said one night. I turned my eyes away. I didn't want him to see how much I agreed.

I agreed so much I knew that I wanted to marry him some day no matter our families, our backgrounds from the country or the city, no matter even about our race. We had our eyes on the future. When I looked at him that evening before he left, I could see there was something on his mind too.

"Too bad you're not black," he said. We laughed because we knew then we were finally telling each other the truth.

Here's something about Louisiana; there's "a nigger in every woodshed." At least that's how my cousin Belinda would say it. She uses the word in the old way. When she says nigger, she means black people most of the time. Except when she is talking about people she likes then she says "negra." That's the way the French used to say it, the ones I am familiar with.

The French used to say "ma petit neg" with such affection that you know they had relatives around them who were black. But for the sake of safety nobody brought that up much. Long time ago, if someone found out that they were just passing for white, they could get strung up. One night somebody would get drunk and grab a rope to kill you, and everybody in the bar would join—because they didn't want to be known as nigger-lovers. That was worse than being black itself.

In my time, people could hang out with their neg friends. They could do business with their negs, and nobody questioned it. But don't go back into history, don't talk politics with them. Then they had to defend the white man with all their hearts.

It was a confused, hard heart that they protected. A couple people in town did their genealogies and they found a Negro who came into their line. That's when they put away their birth certificate and photo albums when you came to visit. They stopped talking about the past and more about QVC and their gardens.

"Don't tell me all of that ancestor stuff, Cynthie," my cousin Jeff said to me. "Let me stay ignorant." He played like it was funny. But it wasn't funny to him or me. I stopped talking about research and school and everything with anyone in my family, except Belinda.

She was the one that told me that my mama was part black. "Why you think you never heard from her again? She loved you that much," she said. "Your paw never forgave her for not telling him. He run her off, but, you know, just because the rest of your family made him."

Belinda told me right before I took off for New Orleans. For years I hated my father. The whole time I was in nursing school.

"Dear Cynthie," his letters went. He never called long distance. "We wonder how you are. Everything fine here. Had a good shrimp season. Had a big party at the house. Miss you. Love, Paw."

I never wrote back, even though I went to visit every few months and stayed in his house. I acted like I never heard a word from him.

Then, one night I confronted him.

Bill is starting to stir.

"Lord have mercy, what's that noise?" he asks me.

"Hello Sweetheart, you were in such a deep sleep I didn't want to disturb you."

"Did I sleep the whole afternoon?"

"It's so nice with me and you here," I say.

"This hurricane, it's really coming?" he asks. "Let's call my family." He picks up the phone, and I see that it was on mute. I had put it that way when he first began sleeping. Now I see we have missed several calls.

"They said they were evacuating. They wanted to know where we are and if we wanted to go with them." He is beginning to shout now. "What is on your mind?"

How could I tell him that I just wanted to stay with him in this room? When I thought about all of the turmoil of my past, and I saw him sleeping there, I just never wanted the day to end.

"I guess the time slipped away from me," I say.

"Have mercy," he started to gain his composure. "Let's call downstairs. Don't you hear the rain beating?"

When I asked my father if he ran my mother away because she was black, he hit me square across the mouth. I was in shock. I did not have words.

I had prepared for all kinds of conversations. I had been studying the right way to talk to him like I had been studying my nursing books, even more. I had done all sorts of family research— looking up her maiden name, finding it on the internet, getting in touch with so many people in so many states, none of them had heard of her, but some of them were colored.

That's when I asked him.

"I raised you, and I protected you. But I don't have to let you put a curse on us," he shouted.

I ran from the room. My mouth was bleeding. I packed up my suitcases. I didn't leave at that moment. I waited until after dinner, after the family had gathered around. They laughed and sang a few songs. I watched because something in me had changed. Then I hitched a ride to the bus station, and I got in New Orleans by morning.

"Dear Cynthie," he wrote. "I know what I did was bad. But I'm not such a bad a person. One day you'll see. Love, Paw."

I wrote, but only after a few months. And I even began talking to him. But not about that. And when Bill came home with me, my father treated me like a nice stranger.

Still, he came to the wedding, and he even had one dance with me. Bill's mother asked the band to prepare the song, "La Jolie Blonde." It was my father's favorite, a zydeco song now, but it was popular on the bayou when he was coming up. People sang it in all kinds of ways.

It was the story of a beautiful woman and a man who wanted her. But she was unattainable. The song has lots of different endings.

My father and I did a slow two step around the floor. I wondered who was the blonde. Me, my mother, or him.

Then Bill cut into the dance, the tempo became slightly faster. He gave the two steps a little jump that was all our own. I was floating.

"Yea, yea, we're still in the room," I heard him talking to his family. He was trying to sound calm. "I know there's a hurricane coming. I know. I was sleeping."

He was laughing then with his family. I wonder what they're finding so funny.

"Yes, it's my honeymoon. No, she was awake," he said, "You can't pick us up? The streets are blocked off. You've got to be kidding."

"Vertical evacuation," he told me when he got off the phone. "My folks tell me that was one of the plans anyway. People stay in hotels so that if the water rises, they will be safe." He pulled me by the waist to get back in the bed with him.

The wind was blowing hard against the windows in the outer room. Every few minutes I heard a thud against the glass. The rain hissed, but I was in heaven.

IV.

M e and Sweet Pea woke up when it was dark-dark. We just listened to the storm. The wind had voices like one hundred people all hollering at once.

"It's like waking the dead," Sweet Pea said to me. And I know she wasn't lying.

The wind screamed sometimes like a woman who lost her children to some molester and she finds out, and she falls on her knees. It howled sometimes like a man who sees his child hit by a car in the street. It was like the church choir seeing hell for the first time, beautiful voices shrieking and rumbling, all together but going in different directions. You could hear ripping and cracking like bodies tore limb from limb.

And then there was that time of quiet, when the eye of the hurricane passed over us. It was unearthy and calm.

Sweet Pea and me got up from where we were laying together so close that you wouldn't know which body belonged to who. And we went to the door, hand-in-hand.

We saw so much destruction, and we knew that there was so much more coming after this silence. Outside was so dark that we didn't see anything when we first opened the door. There was no light anywhere. There were just shadows, some darker than others.

After a time, she pointed out to me that Miss Otis' roof had been blowed off, and the tree come up from Jacks' yard. Somebody's bicycle went through Mrs. Jewel's window and there was a pipe busted a few doors down. The water sprayed into the sky. It caught the starlight like a strange fountain. The stars were hanging in the dark blue.

With the clouds gone in the eye of the storm, it was the most beautiful clear night. You never would have thought anything happened here at all. Sweet Pea told me, "It's like we dreamed it. If we go back to bed maybe it'll go away."

Have you ever seen an old lady behave like a child? It wasn't like she was crazy though, she had that sweetness about her since she was a teenager.

She used to tell me that if you pray hard enough, you will get what you want. She said she had seen her mama walk right into the kitchen weeks after she died. They sat down and had a cup of coffee together. They sang a hymn. Her mama told her the day our son would be born.

I guess now he'll be in California wondering about us. I'm sure he tried to call, but the phones were the first to go down. Even just a little rain and there's no phone or electricity in New Orleans.

"It's like a Third World country," he told me years ago. But it wasn't no never mind to anybody around here.

"We got indoor plumbing," Sweet Pea shouted out that day from the living room to him on the phone.

That day he said, "Daddy, why don't y'all come live with me in California? We've got a big house and the sun is always shining. The kids want to see more of you. Mama can watch her television shows."

"No thank you," Sweet Pea and I said just about at the same time.

California got earthquakes, and people got to go everywhere in the car. Can't even take you a good bus ride. New Orleans has people you know all of your life, and even before meeting them good you know somebody in their families. You might even be related to them. So you all in this together, whatever goes on. With or without lights, electricity, or water. You put together what little you got, and you share.

"At some point, you know, you're going to have to move out of that old house," my son said on the phone.

I looked at Sweet Pea. It would probably be kindness to move her somewhere, maybe even California, before she got too old and disable with just me. But she was so happy. She had a little nest by her soft chair. Her glasses were on the table next to the Bible. Her coffee cup that said MOTHER that someone gave her from church was on the television right in her eye sight. The remote stayed on the seat when she wasn't sitting down. There was the footstool that somebody bought her from Krauss that she knitted a few squares to cover.

For Sweet Pea to move away from here, the light would go out of her. I didn't want to be the one to do that. My son didn't want it either, but he didn't know all that. With the blindness of a young man, he told me again, "At some point, y'all going to need to come out here. Why don't you just come out for a visit?"

When I saw that clear night in the hurricane's eye, and I felt the warm breeze working itself up again, I thought, maybe if I said I needed to go to California, then Sweet Pea would do it for me.

I turned to look at her face. She was staring up at the sky like it was talking to her. The starlight hit her face, and I swear all the oldness fell right off. She looked the same as when I met her.

Sweet Pea told me once of a dream she had when she was tired of getting visions of dead people and premonitions of what was going to happen. She predicted our two babies' deaths, and she took those miscarriages hard. She predicted that her favorite cousin would come visit her long after he was buried. She started to pray then that God would take back this gift.

"I been praying," she told me, "that I don't know nothing no more. I don't want to see what shouldn't be seen."

The next night she went to bed. "I'm afraid to be visited. It's too much pain," she told me before she closed her eyes.

All that night I stayed awake guarding against her dead cousin.

The next morning when I finally got to the table with my body dragging, and my eyes tired and hurting from trying to keep the ghosts out of our bedroom, Sweet Pea looked all happy.

"Well, I guess you got a good night sleep," I told her, not joking at all. Still she laughed.

"My prayers have been answered," she said.

I was ready to take all the credit, keeping my ghost watch.

"Don't be disturbing Sweet Pea," I had told them all night, whispering out to the air. "If you like her that much, leave her alone."

I knew that I had kept her cousin away by giving him a good talking to.

But before I got out my bragging, Sweet Pea related to me this dream she had. Her cousin came into her mind. He appeared as he did when he was young. His face was clean-shaven. His eyes were clear. He had a brightness about him everywhere as if there was a spotlight on him.

And both of us were there, her and me, she said. But we looked like we had been dipped in ashes. We were gray, and so was the place we sat at the table. She was more gray then me, and I was gray enough, the color of one of the statues in City Park, she told me. We were having a regular conversation, but it was like he was alive, and we were the dead ones.

"After that, I just don't think anyone else is coming to visit," she said. "I think he brought the last message."

"That is?" I asked.

"That what we think is living actually ain't," she said, perfectly pleased with herself.

"I think you must be right," I told her, "because I sure don't feel alive right now. I'm dead on my feet."

That morning she gave me my usual good breakfast. But different this time, she sent me back to bed, not to do any of the many things she had saved up for me around the house. I did not need to unclog the bathroom drain, put a washer in the sink faucet, fix that board that squeaked when she walked on it, bring her to the plant nursery.

She put me in bed like a baby that day.

"Living is not really for us," she said, "We just passing the time. Might as well spend it one way or another." She added, "Make yourself happy."

That was a few years ago, and since then not a day went by that Sweet Pea didn't tell me a joke or a story that tickled my fancy. It was if her young self came back, the one that, when we met, was always flirting with me.

That's why, as the eye of the storm finished passing over and we went back to bed, I held her real tight against my body. It was as if I wanted to tell her, you and I, we are together through everything. Like the vows we took when we were young and didn't know anything. Now the words they put in our mouths finally came true. We cleaved together in the body, but also somewhere way deeper.

Then, the wind started whipping around the house again and calling in its demon chorus. The house shook. Tree branches were hitting the outside walls all around us. Every few minutes Sweet Pea would catch her breath. "Jesus," she'd say not too loud but like calling on Him.

Then it happened. We started to see the water. So fast it came up to the side of the bed. Then before we could hardly sit up, it was in the bed with us. We were trying to pull our legs over the side, but already our legs were floating. Sweet Pea's nightgown was coming up to her chest. I saw her body was gray. I was holding on to her tight. The furniture around us started floating around the room.

The chifferobe started to tilt and fall. Sweet Pea's dressing table went wobbling off. I got her to stand on top of the bed finally. I couldn't figure out what to do next. It was like Noah without the Ark. I heard screaming cats and the sound of something much bigger outside the house. I looked over at the windows and the water was even higher outside.

"My God, Sweet Pea," I told her. "We going to have to swim." One thing I know about her, she was a good swimmer.

We quick-tied our clothes together so that the water could not make us drift apart. Then Sweet Pea and I pushed off the bed. We head for the opening to the attic where the staircase was. When she asked me to build it, we both thought this is for storage. We never imagined using it like this. We got as far as the pull-down stair. Sweet Pea was treading while I yanked on the rope and the ladder fell down. When I went to pull on the pajamas to bring her close to me, a table floated between us. Her head was down.

I pushed the table away from me. I pulled on the pajamas harder. She was underwater still. I pulled hard and I was getting her as my one foot stood on the ladder and my arm was holding on while the other brought Sweet Pea over to me. I pulled and suddenly the pajamas were light. The fabric ripped. In the dark, hell, damn dark of the house, I could not see Sweet Pea.

I dove off the ladder. I went swimming underwater in the dark house. I kept bumping into all kind of things. Sweet Pea's chair. The cork picture frames. All sorts of odd things that you don't realize have air in them.

"Oh my God, please save my baby," I was praying. The water was just getting higher and pushier. There was a real current now that had broken through the dining room window and was exiting out of the door. I was trying to swim, then, I thought I was going to drown. But the Lord didn't have that in mind.

"Lord Have Mercy. Lord Have Mercy." The water pushed me right through the front door on to my neighbor's porch. I didn't want to hold on. But something inside of me said to me, "What if Sweet Pea is alive and she comes looking for you?" That's the only thought that kept me clinging to the ironwork on the porch, and then, after the water got higher, that got me grabbing on to the branches of fallen trees.

I was able to find a way through the front port of my neighbor's attic and sat under her roof until I guess I fell to sleep. When I woke up, the wind had passed and the sky was bright.

V.

I always wanted to come to the Superdome but not like this. The night was like going to hell. And it's still going on.

At first, we settled into the good seats and figured we'd have dinner and enjoy each other's company like we did at home. The baby was tired from all the running around. So after Andra walked him up and down the steps a few times, he fell asleep in her lap.

Then Mama took out dinner, and we ate potato salad and fried chicken. She saw an old man looking hungry not too far from us, and she gave him a stuff bell pepper that she had saved for later. We drank the water we brought, and then we went to the fountain. That's when we saw the mess.

The water was splashed around the fountain just like at the public school football games. But this time, there wasn't anyone to fix it or clean it up. The bathrooms were even worse. It was like nobody remembered that people needed tissue paper if they were going to spend the night.

Mama said that she'd just hold until morning. But that didn't work. So Andra had to take her to go pee in a jar on the side of the empty seats. It was already feeling hellish. Then the wind started hollering like a pack of dogs. Children around us were crying and men were saying, "Shit" out loud.

When the tiles started to rip off the roof and we could see the sky, everybody got quiet, except for the whimpering. From somewhere in the dome, we could see the television people were taking pictures. That was the only light. And then that went out. We were sitting in the dark holding on to one another and praying.

Mama apologized. "We should have gone home," she told me.

"No," I told her, "This ain't nothing."

Morning come and here we are. It's quiet outside, and everybody feel like they been to hell and back, so we going toward the doors.

They tell us we can't get out. They got National Guard all around the ring of the building. They got rifles. Somebody shout, "Since when we become criminals?"

The National Guard close that heavy door from the lobby to the outside walkway. It sounds like the door of a jail cell.

I tell Andra and Mama to sit where they are. I go walking around the edges of the dome, all around the garage places where the cars pull the celebrities inside. The elevator isn't working, so I sneak down the stairwell. I go to a door that I think gets out and I push on it. I am face-to-face with a boy about 10 years younger than me. He has a high-powered rifle.

His face is already pale, but it goes white when he sees me. He puts the rifle butt against his shoulder. "Halt!" he tells me.

"You got my attention," I tell him. I'm trying to be cool as can be. These could be my last words. "Listen. I'm just trying to get some fresh air." It's the first thing I say because, damn, the air is fresh compared to the dark stink we been in. "You don't shoot people for trying to get air, do you?" I say it with a smile in my voice. I am trying to be so cool. I don't think he can hear the trembling, but I do.

He lowers the gun. He still has his finger on the trigger.

"Really man. Don't shoot me for trying to get air in my own home town."

He relaxes a little, and the gun goes down by his side.

"Don't that feel better?" I smile

"Yes, sir."

He must be about 18. Looks like somebody at my job's baby brother.

"How old you are?"

"Twenty, sir."

"Don't need to call me sir. I'm not that much older than you," I tell him this, but I know I'm older from experience. "Do you have children?"

"No, sir. I mean, no."

"I got my wife and mama and baby upstairs. And it's a stinking mess. Would you want your mama in there?"

He tells me, "Never." He's relaxed now because he's telling the truth.

"How come they not letting us out of here?" I ask.

"Just orders. That's all I know."

"Come on. Get real. How come?"

"They don't want people looting."

"I got my family in there. We don't loot. The refrigerator is full at home and the beer is cold."

"No, sir. Maybe not," he tells me.

"What do you mean?" I'm about to get insulted. This boy doesn't know me. Then he tells me to follow him. I'm not on the ground as I thought. I'm a few floors up on the ramp. I walk outside with him. All I see is National Guard white boys all over, all with guns, all looking just as hot and scared as this one in the midday sun. Then I look down, where this boy is pointing to me. I look down past the ramp to the city. It is blue-green like the surface of the lake.

VI.

The hotel started sending everyone out to the street because the French Quarter is dry. They said they don't want to be responsible. I don't know where we will go. Some people say we can still get in the Superdome. Others say near the Convention Center there will be buses to pick us up. Bill is still trying to get in touch with his family.

Family is everything to him now. That seemed to come over him while we waited for the storm to clear. Suddenly, I wasn't family. I was more like a stranger.

You find out a lot about a person in an emergency. Bill started to change as the windows started to shake in the hotel. He never told me anything bad about myself before this evening.

As the night wore on and we heard the windows breaking in the suite, he got more and more afraid. We moved with the other hotel guests to the building's center, the ballroom. When we were lying on the ballroom floor, Bill blamed me for not waking him up. Of course, I was wrong, and I apologized. Over and over, I apologized. But that didn't seem to be enough.

I don't know what he was looking for. He wanted me to make it all better, I suspected, like his mother did. "Wait up, Bill," I wanted to tell him, "I didn't have a mother to dry my tears. So it's best if you just be a man."

Did I say that? No, but I thought it. And then I began to wonder—what did my mother have to do with anything?

I remembered what Belinda told me, "Don't go thinking nothing about this now I told you your Maman was black. It don't mean nothing no way." She said, "It's just going to make you miserable. Thinking you don't belong to the people who love you. Hating yourself. Not being satisfied with anything."

At the time, I thought she was talking about being black. But now I think she was talking just about me. Because here I am now in the hotel with Bill acting like a spoiled child, and I am behaving like a wimp, just asking his forgiveness. As if I had something to be really sorry for. I didn't bring on the hurricane.

There were no bellmen, so we had to carry our own bags, and when we got outside, he handed me mine. "See if you can be responsible for this one thing," he said.

Instead of answering him, I walked in a different direction from him. I walked straight down Bourbon Street to the French Market while he stood on Canal Street with his mouth wide open.

"Where in the hell do you think you're going?" he asked..

"Do you know where you're going?" I replied.

"No."

"Well then," I said, "You think you're the only one with a problem. Look around."

"Wait!" he said again.

"I told you that I was sorry. Now what are you going to do with that?" I shouted.

And then it came over both of us. A huge sense of relief. We were arguing in the street, in a city where buildings might lay in pieces, where people looked desperate and confused, where men and women were crying and wandering. We were arguing. And blessed that we had someone to argue with.

I dropped my suitcase. It went into a puddle of water. I flew into his arms. We laughed. We cried. We laughed again. Then like conspirators, we thought about where we could break and enter to get food and a bed, and how could we reach his family so they knew we were okay, and when would we talk to my father to tell him that love had kept us safe and was enough for us, and that we even loved him. Bill and I walked through the French Quarter. The air was still. The streets were quiet and intimate. After a night of howling wind and rain, the city was surprisingly dry.

VII.

From the porthole of the attic, I see what Sweet Pea had read to me in the Bible about the flood in the Old Testament. It took everything. It didn't matter whether the people were good or bad. If they just weren't Noah's family, God flooded them out. So I think God is wrong. I never thought that before, but I think that now. He is wrong to take the good people and bad at the same time. But Sweet Pea never would have doubted God. So, I try to believe, for her sake. Maybe if I believe, she'll show up.

I have looked for Sweet Pea in every direction since I woke. My eyes hurt from the brightness of the sun and the water. I feel drunk the heat is in my head so bad. I feel like fire is under my skin. When I look out at the water all under and around this house, I don't see anything but the tops of trees. I see dead animals.

I even try to get out and swim a little to get some wetness on my body. But there is a current going who knows where. I just dip in and I can feel it pulling me already. So I pull back into the window and then I'm exhausted for most of the day.

I wake up to the sounds of men calling, "Anybody here?" Their voices are the only living things out here. There are no birds even. "Anybody out here?" They are not far from this house.

I get up from the floor of the attic, and I go to the porthole window, and I wave.

They pick me up, give me water, and we boat to the interstate. They leave me there in a lump.

It is hotter on the highway than in the house. Someone puts his shirt over my back and the top of my head. I lay down on the pavement, and I wait. Next to me is a woman making a racket, whistling like a bird and going "Da-da." I heard people telling her that the city will come pick us up. So I rest my mind. The priest from Corpus Christi is here. People around me say let him give me the Last Rites.

"Sacrament of Reconciliation," he says.

Then he begins.

I repent all my sins from the things I did to the things I didn't do and should have, the people I hurt, and the people I could have helped and didn't, and I ask for help from God and all of his Saints.

While I am praying with the skinny little white priest, he turns into Sweet Pea. I can feel my whole body smile. It's like taking off an overcoat. I feel cool. She puts her big, soft arms around me, and we hold one another. I'm holding her now. She's old but she smells like she was pretty and young. She makes my heart feel calm.

I'm holding her and feeling like I'm having the best dream when I hear someone behind me say, "There goes another one."

Then I hear nothing.

VIII.

We fight not to get on the bus. People are lining everyone up, and soldiers are saying men over to the left and women to the right.

I tell my family that we should keep dropping back in the line farther and farther. I can see Andra is wondering whether this is the right thing. But she doesn't say anything. She just holds on to the baby. It means that we will stay in the filthy Superdome longer. Maybe in the dark for a few more days. But I told her and Mama what I saw, all of New Orleans is under. So where are we going anyway?

We sit back in the Superdome seats and the National Guard boy sees me. We're some of the few left. He tells me to follow him, and bring the family. At the back of the Superdome, I see a line of people with children and wives. They are going together. They are mostly white people. I didn't even see them in the Superdome. I don't know whether to curse him or to be happy.

He sees my face.

"I'm sorry," he says. I think he has tears in his eyes. But I don't stop long enough to look hard. I just say, "Thanks, man." I put my hand on his shoulder, and he jumps slightly. I notice it, but I can't take time to process it. I hold Andra and Mama by the hand. Andra is holding the baby tight. We get in the line of families. I hear somebody ask where we are going. "Don't know, M'am," the National Guardsman says. She looks like she's about to get salty with him and say something like, "You don't know?" But she changes her mind, gets in line, and on the bus fast. I think from her accent that she was probably a tourist.

We get on the bus, and Andra sits close under my arm while Mama holds the baby. Thank God for the baby or we'd all be falling apart. Andra is praying very softly as we leave New Orleans. I'm thinking about my home. I don't know where we're going or if we're ever coming back.

IX.

Bill's family works for the city, and we run into one of them while we are walking. His cousin is going back to a boat that he brought from home. He was pulling people out of the water and putting them on dry land. He sends us to a hotel not far from the Convention Center where the lights aren't working, but there are supplies. We get four bottles of water from a case, then we put them back. We each take one after we learn that the police and firemen are running low.

No one seems to notice us as they work all around. As we're sitting, we hear rumors that no one knows what to do, and no one in authority can be found. Someone jokes, "Where's Waldo?"

I ask if I can help with any patients, and they send me with armed guards to the Riverwalk next to the Convention Center. "Do you think all this fire power is necessary?" I am being sarcastic.

No one looks at me when I say this. The police in the car stare straight ahead. We are going through roads I've never seen in back of the business district. We pass all the new hotels near the Warehouse District. There are so many hotels in New Orleans that everyone could have come inside during the storm. Strange that they put people out on the street when everyone knows that insurance will reimburse them for their losses.

I don't see anyone on these streets, although most of the time this area is full of the new people who have come into the city—the art dealers, the music scouts, the conventioneers, and business people who know the way to make money. In New Orleans, there are lots of colleges, but few jobs outside of oil and management for whites, politics and service industry for blacks. Only the Catholic and private schools teach college prep courses anyway. The city makes sure that most of the public school kids are educated only so far as to make beds and bus tables.

Finally, in the cop car, when we take the overpass, I see the city underwater. It looks like the lake has taken over.

"It's even worse downriver," one cop says.

I realize then I have hardly thought about my extended family downriver. They evacuated to Saint Bernard. Buras is now surely part of the Gulf.

"You heard anything about the cities near the Gulf, like Buras?" I ask.

"You looking at the Mouth of the Gulf here," one laughs.

I don't want them to see me cry, so I bite my lip and pray under my breath.

The police drop me off at the Convention Center where the street is crowded with people. The sick are strewn across the ground. Nearby are dead bodies. "Don't have to carry them too far," someone explains who seems to have taken charge. Another person is arguing with him that this is not a good plan. I walk away from both of them.

But there is very little difference here between the dead and the living. Some of the dead still sit in the wheelchairs that their

186

family used to roll them here. One man tells me he stayed in the city because his grandmother was so old that she might not have survived the trip in the car. "Now look," he says. She is covered with a sheet. But he sees through it, I'm sure, to her last terrible grimace in death.

Some people lay on the sidewalk asking for food. I have a package of crackers in my pocket left from one of my hotel meals. I give it to a young woman, and she takes it as if it is something gourmet. She shares it with her daughters, who give a few crumbs to the people next to them. One of the men refuses. "No thanks," he says and turns in another direction. I can hear his stomach rumble from here.

I see an old man with tears running down his face, and I tell him, "It's going to be OK soon." But I see few personnel except for a police car every once in a while. The cops look as if they are going to burst if someone asks them another question.

A little girl comes to tell me that she and her family had tried to walk across the Mississippi River Bridge out of the flooded city, but helicopters began flying low over them and shooting at them. Her mother said the helicopters were kicking up dirt and rocks. For safety, she brought her daughter into the bushes alongside the bridge. It did make them feel that the authorities wanted them dead.

"No, baby," I told the child, "No one would hurt you. They've got no reason."

Her grandmother lay on the sidewalk nearby. I could hear her grunt when I said this.

Now I look out at the sea of black faces. I think about the question my Paw asked me before I got married, "This what you signing up for? To live poor like them?"

I told him that Bill's family was actually better off than we were.

"Don't make no difference," he said.

Now, I can see that it does and it doesn't.

Bill's relatives are in a nice hotel—as nice as it gets today. But they are on the telephone and riding around the city, trying to help in every way. They are making plans to get people rescued, talking to one another about where they can get food, cars, and boats. They know almost everyone in the city. Bill says they've known one another's families for generations. "We've always taken care of each other. How do you think we got anywhere?"

Now, they are working alongside white people, helping and organizing and talking to them no different than Paw talks to his neighbor. I wish he could see that. He had said, "Never in this world" when I asked him if people might change in the future to accept one another. He said, "They came from Africa, and we were their masters."

He forgot for a moment that my mother was black. And that time, I had looked at him and said, "What about me?"

"I raised you so you wouldn't know the other side."

It was then that I realized that not knowing was a choice. If I thought white, I could say that I didn't know about the problems of blacks. It must have been God's decision to make them poor, hungry, jobless, or they had done something wrong to bring pain to themselves. I could feel safe.

Now, I look at the people in the street, all of the faces, and I think how many of them did something bad enough to deserve this. Or how many were shunned along the way by people like my Paw— good people who knew better and didn't do anything to change.

And it makes me think, as I am holding back tears and running to get the little supplies that we have to treat the sick, that I made the right choice.

I married up when I married Bill, not because of my color— because of my heart.

Someone calls out that the city has dropped off another body from the interstate. It is an old man. "Look at this," people gather around.

"He's smiling and he's hugging himself," someone says. "Heatstroke makes people do funny things."

I look at the old man's face. It seems strangely familiar.

For some reason, I think about the hotel where I got married and all the hotels within a few blocks radius. There are thousands of rooms. They are all empty. I wonder, why aren't we all inside?

The Value of a Life

I spotted the body that had washed up against the bottom of the fence. Plastic bags, pieces of wood and tin, a tricycle, and a kitchen pot were lying alongside of the corpse like they were all caught in a sink strainer when the flood drained out. This wire fence—a hurricane fence at that—and others like it, accumulated these strange collections of debris at the edge of every lot in the Ninth Ward like the junk I see at the bottom of my kid's toy box. This is what God leaves when He's tired of playing with us. Your mind has to have some kind of explanation.

When I first saw the body, I wasn't with anyone from the ladder truck. I had just dropped off a civilian on the interstate, and I had carried my boys from the fire station to the steps of the hotel where we're set up. They had all been through the wringer for the past week since the flood, and it showed on their faces. Nobody was talking anymore. Their eyes were round like zombies. The only thing they could do was to sit with the food that we took from the store, open the cartons and bags on their laps, and eat.

But I couldn't sit down with them yet. So even though they

told me not to go, and even when my boy Johnny volunteered to come along, I left alone.

Nobody got up to stop me when they heard my pickup truck start up. Johnny threw up his hand and waved goodbye, without even looking in my direction.

Most of the time, once we came home to the firehouse together, we'd settle down and cook, sit around the table, and laugh. But not lately. Walking through empty neighborhoods looking for any living person changed everything. Now at night, we were as still as the stale air in the closed up hotel where we slept. Our bunkmates were as awkward as strangers.

Even my own skin felt rubbery and strange, always clammy and cool. I felt like I was in the body of an alien. Put a gun to my head and shoot, and something like Styrofoam or clay would fall out in a lump to the floor.

I just had to escape tonight because I was getting unsure about whether I was dead or alive. I wanted to drive a little while before sundown.

I headed back down into the Lower Nine because I needed to see the place where I grew up after the water rushed in.

The bridge over the Industrial Canal was steep, and all I saw was blue sky as I climbed my truck up. But the road came down like a slide into Hell.

There was mud covering the road, and my truck tires spun as I came off the bridge. There were no stop signs, no lights, and no traffic. So I just skidded onto what I guessed was the street.

It was actually hard to find my block. I had to look for landmarks—the top of some construction near the Intracoastal Waterway or a piece of old building. Houses were pushed into the street or on top of one another.

That's when I saw the body. It was caught on one of the many standing hurricane fences. Unlike the pretty, wood, privacy fences that people put up around their houses and the wind flattened in an instant, the open wire fences stayed up. The water just ran through them. But they collected every bit of life.

At first I couldn't tell that it was a body. It was bloated and laid to the side like a piece of felled tree. It was swollen, brown, black and purple depending on the way the light hit. The figure was slimy, mashed in places like rotten fruit—black on the outside with a reddish core. There were plastic bags from Sav-A-Center somewhere around what were probably the knees. There was a piece of something, maybe rope or mud-covered clothing, hanging from it like a tail, and cutting through the swollenness in the center.

If I hadn't seen dogs and cats dead like this all week, I would have thrown up just then. But I held myself. I heaved a little, and I guess I was saved because I hadn't eaten in a long while. When I started to approach the body, the stench was even worse than the stink in the rest of the city. Death smells like rotten eggs, oil, and garbage stirred up with rotten meat.

The flies started to swarm around me as I got closer to the fence. I had mostly gotten used to them by now. But they were worse over here. So I got in my truck to go back to my boys.

After I started driving, I realized that I had not tagged the body. But maybe I wouldn't. What was the use?

The news wasn't worth sharing when I returned to my men. Everything was news now. All of it bad. The movie theater where we used to sit in the balcony and make out with our girlfriends had fallen—the roof to the slab. The jazz joint where we drank in high school had water up to the ceiling, and the owner had drowned. They found him surrounded by broken bottles of liquor.

We had spent our childhoods pitching pennies and smoking our first cigarettes behind one another's garages, all gone now, slid off their foundations from the rushing water and washed into grimy mush. We had been helping each other to build new homes before Katrina so we could live with our fiancés, wives and young children in the same neighborhood. The construction now looked as ragged as the old houses where we were raised.

And my friends were used up. Before the storm, when the fire call bell was rare, I had sat around and shared with the others— telling them that my wife was thinking of leaving me those two times, that we only got married because she was pregnant, that my baby was born and it was something they should never see, that my daddy died after we hadn't spoken in weeks or maybe never about anything important. My boys at work now were actually better than my family.

Johnny was the best among them. We sat elbow-to-elbow so many nights after the storm. The first few times, I think, just to keep away the feeling of being alone. After spending the days wading through water neck high, we checked each other at night for leeches.

Before the storm, Johnny came looking for me just after dark before he made the rounds for happy hour at the local joints and before sunrise when he was ready to go fishing. He taught me how to bait for bass, dive under the boat to untie a shrimp net, and to keep my mouth shut around women.

He told me about the time he went hunting and thought he shot a buck. But when he walked close to it with his knife, he found out that the buck was just stunned, and they began to tangle.

I was laughing so hard that I almost spilled my beer as he described being flung over the horns, being butted and kicked until he finally got to the buck's underside and stabbed him in the heart. The proof of his kill was the carcass Johnny drove home across his truck hood, the antlers on his wall, and the deer sausages he brought to everyone on the holidays.

I started to tell my wife the story, and she stopped me.

"I can't hear it. It's too brutal," she said.

"You like those sausages, don't you?" I asked her.

"Sure."

"Well, it don't come from the superstore," I said.

She shrugged.

I think she just doesn't get a lot of things.

Like she tells my son to come kiss me every time I come home. I tell him, "Give me five, man."

Later, I told her, "What are you trying to do to him?"

She said, "He needs to be able to show affection."

"Christ." I just walked out of the room.

Let him learn to be a man.

Every day, we get up early at the firehouse. We hose the truck, the floor, the sidewalk. We fix the tools and see what needs replacing. We throw on gear, do jumps and climbs, and time ourselves with a stopwatch. We carry weight up and down ladders for the time when we will have to go into a burning building and pull out people who have gotten smoke inhalation. And we study the way fire will curl near the ceiling and lick at the top of your head, taunt you and threaten to peel off your flesh, and then how to go into that building, being afraid, but ready to battle with axes and hoses, and just sheer will.

It was strange that the first emergency I had was pulling up someone who had drowned in the lake. He was an out-of-towner who drove too fast and went off the road near the lakefront airport.

When I'm with my boys at the station house, they understand. Too much, maybe. So I didn't tell them about the body. I just couldn't.

The next morning, it was a sizzling 90 degrees before we even got out of the hotel good. We had one assignment after another, all of them related to the flood and recovery—trying to get the hydrants to work in the middle of the city, trying to see if the few trucks in some of the stations still operated, trying to find out how much gear we had in total. Looking for our other men.

Some of them, yellow-bellied as the day they were born,

took off as soon as they found out that a serious hurricane was coming. Others of them chose their families over their oath. Some lost their minds when the flood happened. On the morning after the storm, more ran to safety, to their houses outside the city. But that's when the shit got really bad.

There's not a lot of loyalty to New Orleans, except among the people born in New Orleans. The men who stayed were a combination of generations born on this land, and those who still cared for the people who had no choice but to live here.

Who would live here when the shooting goes on day and night, and the buses never pass on time, and no one can get a civil servant on the telephone—except during the hour between 10:30 and 11:00, or 3:30 and 4:00—when they still talk to you like you're interrupting their lunch and dinner plans? Only the people who love New Orleans and can't help themselves. Usually one and the same.

They are the ones who sit on their porches at night with a hand fan and wearing their slippers, laughing over old stories, and telling lies. They spend their last dollar on an ostrich feather for a costume. Even if they have 11 children, they will put a plate on the table for you when you visit their houses and insist you eat.

They stay home to take care of their sick mamas and HIV brothers. They bring their diabetic sisters to their doctors' appointments. They wait for hours at the Department of Motor Vehicles without reading a newspaper, so as not to be rude to one another.

They can't help themselves, and somebody has to stay with them.

When the work was done for the day, and the guys decided tonight after dinner we should expropriate hot beer from the grocery store, I took off in my truck. It nagged me that I didn't tag that body, even though we'll probably never find an identity.

One of these new experts that seem to be popping up all over town gave me some advice recently. He said to me, "One of your biggest fears should be disease."

"Thank you," I told him.

Who here doesn't know already that New Orleans is one of the disease capitals of the United States? Mosquitos, yellow fever, equine fever, meningitis. I've lived here all of my life, and sickness comes around every year. He's a scientist, so he doesn't know that medicine is not where we put our faith.

My grandmother used to make the sign of the cross on my forehead every day before I walked out of the house. She stood cooking in the kitchen for at least an hour before my mother got up and helped to get the little ones dressed. My grandmother took me to the sink, ran the faucet, and made the cross on my head with tap water. She said it was as good as holy water if you didn't have any.

She did have some, but she kept it on the altar in our house for special occasions. The altar had candles, saint pictures, and framed photographs of dead relatives. In the middle was a big, crystal decanter with a crucifix hung by a string around the bottle's neck. The bottle always stayed dusty, maybe because of the way the air circulated in our house. I remember that there was always a shaft of light coming from a window across the hall that settled on the bottle. In the stream of light were visible specks of dust. I stirred my hand in the light and the dust swirled.

At night, the holy candle that my grandmother lit at the altar would send tiny triangles of light from the cut-glass bottle into the rooms off the hall like little flames settling on the beds and the walls.

She said I was always protected, and I believed her until I was about 12 years old.

That year, an old lady neighbor called some of us kids to the porch to go to the grocery store for her, and when we returned instead of giving us money—we were hoping for change—she said she would give us advice.

"The devil has the power," she said.

We stared. A couple of kids started to back off the porch.

"The devil could take and throw this house up in the air and make it crash to the ground. Matchsticks," she said and tossed her hands up and jittered her fingers to show something had been broken to pieces.

"Oh, yeah," this boy from the corner joined in, "my mama told me that."

"But you don't know, you. Unless you seen it." She continued, "I saw it myself one afternoon. I was lying in the bed and listening to the rain, and my eyes was closed. And the sun came moving through my room, and all I could see was a red ball over my eyelids. And then the raindrops was running down the insides of my eyes, red raindrops. And then I jump up off of my bed, and look out the window, and I seen blood rain."

Everybody on the porch gasped.

"Is you momma ever seen blood rain?" she asked the boy.

He shook his head, no.

I watched her talk as she took a deep breath and seemed to get bigger. "Is the devil himself that make the clouds and the thunder. God don't want thunder. And lightening is what hurts people. And God don't want no hurt to nobody. But the devil got power, so you got to respect him," she added.

She got up and shuffled slowly inside her house while we waited silently, afraid that she would hear anything we said. She returned with two statues—one was St. Joseph. The other was somebody spearing the devil under his feet.

"This what you got to do. Pray to St. Joseph. Pray to the Archangel Michael," she said, then, she reached in her pocket. "Drop this powder over your head, then on your floor." It was a brown powder that stank a little bit, something like the old woman.

"This here graveyard dust and something else I got," she laughed. "Put some on."

Most of the children jumped back. But I moved toward her

so she could sprinkle a little of it on me.

"Now, you safe," she said.

Some of the kids wouldn't come near me after that.

Now, I wondered what happened to that old lady. The devil may have gotten her by now. Everything around us was graveyard dust.

Was it good dust or bad dust? Research that, I would say to the scientist.

I finally found the place where the body was still on the ground. But this time, when I approached it, I wore my Hazmat suit. I didn't want flies on me. They were too much for my skin these days. Something about me had changed—the flies and mosquitoes usually can't bite through my thick skin enough to get satisfaction.

Whenever we go hunting or fishing, the flies and mosquitoes will be eating up the friend next to me. But they light on my arm, then, just fly off.

"Man, why they don't never get you?" a new guy with us one time asked me. "You putting something on your arms?"

"No, man," I told him I wasn't using any kind of repellent, "I'm just beautiful like that. They don't want to mark me up."

The guys in the boat laughed.

"Beautiful, my ass," Johnny responded. That started another round of ass jokes among the others.

Out here in this quiet though, with the sun about to go down, and everything around me destroyed, I began to wonder: Why don't mosquitoes bite me? And why do some things happen to some people and not others?

The voice of Johnny in my head said, "Stop thinking, fool. Go do what you got to do."

I followed these instructions like the clay man that I am.

I put on the Hazmat suit next to the truck. I covered my head and my hands too. I couldn't hardly see anything then, and I was burning up hot. But I lugged over to the body. I was just supposed to tag it and move on, so somebody could come back for it. But I had to move away the paper and trash to do that.

Then something told me to look at it hard. I didn't feel right just tagging it and not giving it some kind of respect. So I looked at the body near to where the rope was tied, and I realized that I was looking at the back. I turned it over, and it was not as awful as you'd think. It was the face of an old woman, smashed and caked with mud. The features were over to one side, and she had either a grimace or a smile. I could not tell. Her gray hair was washed across her forehead and wrapped part way around her neck.

I turned her back to the ground, and I looked around to see any landmarks, so I could describe her location.

There was nothing but sky all above me, and, as far as I could see, common destruction.

I took off the Hazmat suit at my pickup, and I looked toward the old lady's body up against the fence. I felt bad again suddenly, so I quickly steeled myself. Tonight, I'd go home and tell the guys about the body. And I'd tell them I tagged it. I got into my truck, turned the ignition. The car didn't start.

"Shit," I tried turning the engine over and over. I knew the problem: the alternator. I had used up the battery yesterday by shining my headlights on the street ahead of the hotel, just so we could feel a little bit more normal. And I hadn't charged it up enough, and now it was lifeless.

Luckily, I had water in the back of the truck. So I wouldn't die of heatstroke. But nobody knew where I was. The cell phones hadn't worked since the storm. So here I was.

Nobody was around. I might just have to walk.

But not tonight.

The sun was starting to go down, and despite all the destruction around me, the sky still was clear and striped from blue to purple. It was damn beautiful.

The air stank. I could hear stray dogs beginning to howl. The landscape was just forms in the distance, and shadows began to grow into dark forms nearby.

The sun was descending fast. I got in my car.

I looked through the glove compartment. There was nothing to eat, but it was filled with pennies.

My son had started to collect coins. At first, all kinds of coins. He was looking at the dates of every one. The newer they were, the more he prized them. He kept a jar near his bed. Anything before 1995, he considered too old to keep.

The jar was about half full when my wife discovered it.

She was cleaning under the bed, and she felt something hard when she passed the broom. She tried to fish it out with the broom, but it was too heavy. So she had to crawl on her belly and grab it with her hand.

My son came into the room then, she told me. He began to bounce on the bed while she was under it. He thought that was funny. She was squawking and hollering at him, until finally he understood it wasn't a joke.

To punish him, she said she was going to keep his penny jar.

When I got home, he was sitting in his room, too angry to come out.

"Mama stole my money," he told me.

"Mamas don't steal," I told him. "They always have a good reason, and you can't say that. It's blasphemy."

"Mama got my money jar," he changed the words but not his tone.

When she told me how she had disciplined him, I had to agree. We couldn't let the mischief in him take over. But then I didn't agree about how she was going to resolve it.

"I think he should give the money to the poor," she told me.

"But it's his coin collection," I said.

"Which is more important—teaching him or satisfying him?" she asked.

"Well, you know what is. But does he have to pay for it? Can't we just give him some money to donate to the poor?" I asked.

"You make the choice," she said, and she left.

That night he and I had a long talk.

"Sometimes you do something wrong. Sometimes you're just in the wrong place at the wrong time," I said.

"I got to give my money to the poor?" he asked, "You making me?"

I still wondered myself if the punishment was too harsh.

"Being good is really important," I told him. I had to back up his mother now, "Yea. You've got to give it."

"It's not fair," he said.

I pretended not to hear.

Grudgingly, he went to church the next week and dropped all his pennies into the poor box, and his mother now put a poor box at the door so we could drop all of our change.

Once in a while she would see him collecting things out of the sofa cushions, and she'd make him throw the change into the poor box. But I noticed that he was squirreling away pennies everywhere now. I found them in the toes of his sneakers, in his bottom drawer, and here in the ashtray of the truck.

I waited for a while and tried the engine again, but no dice. The sun was going down and I was starting to smell the night stench. The humidity in the evening soaked into the rot and made it worse. The stray dogs were howling closer.

I curled up inside the truck.

It was too dark and quiet to go to sleep. So I found my eyes staying open after sunset. The broken houses and trees, fallen on their sides, loomed like blacker black against black.

It was silent outside. I cracked the windows, but the stench was so bad, I did better with the windows up, even if it was hot and smothering inside the truck cab.

It was then, maybe around midnight, that I saw it.

It looked like a black red cloud. It formed behind the other clouds that blanketed the sky. I could tell that the sky was cloudy because the stars were not visible, and then suddenly, I'd see plenty of them. Then this black-red cloud came across the sky, but instead of going the way of the others, riding the wind from left to right. It seemed to descend down to earth, making a red glow of the entire horizon, and then it came nearer.

I must be dreaming, I thought. But I knew where I was— in the truck near the body, somewhere in the Ninth Ward.

Soon, the truck too was enveloped in this black-red fog. For some reason, I felt cold. And I started to pray.

"Holy Mary, Mother of God, pray for us now and at the hour of our death," I said.

I could hear the stray dogs close to the car. They were bumping against the doors. There must have been 20 of them.

Stray dogs were a problem even before the hurricane. People would be picnicking in City Park, then, a pack of dogs would come up. Their instincts had made them like wolves. They would head for the picnic food and tear off with the sandwiches and a whole ham or turkey.

People couldn't fight back. The dogs would go into attack. Most of the time, people just backed off and went home disgusted.

Why didn't anything go right? Dogs killing people. People killing people. And now Katrina. What was God thinking?

I put my head down and prayed, "God why don't you like us? We pray all the time. We do the right thing. We try to take care of our poor people. We are the poor people."

I remembered that my grandmother remained in her house

over the years as her community became ragged, and her neighbors grew poorer and poorer.

"It's time to leave," my mother told her.

"I'm not getting out of my home," she responded.

The drug addicts got worse, and her next door neighbor was murdered by a crackhead.

Everybody in the neighborhood knew who he was. They talked about him at the funeral.

Then, he showed up and went to pray in front of the casket.

The police caught him, and one of them asked, "Why did you come here?"

"She was like my mother," he answered.

A sick mind has no fear.

I remembered the body against the fence. The dogs would make mincemeat out of her. They would pull off her skin from her bones. She had brought me here, kept me here, and I couldn't desert her. I took an old baseball bat that I had in the car. I threw open the door and I began to shout.

"I-yi-yi," I screamed the words my grandmother used on her deathbed. I swung the baseball bat as hard as I could in every direction.

The air was thick and red. The dogs growled. I felt the bat crack one or two of them in the skull. I really couldn't see. But I kept screaming and swinging. I finally heard the dogs scatter.

I went back into the car. The red cloud was still there. I felt sick.

Shortly before the sun rose, my vision returned a little. The air was still thick but white now from the fog. A fine mist, glowing with light, soaked me through when I got out of the cab. I washed my face in it. I took off my shirt and wiped myself—over my head, and down my neck and back.

I returned to the truck until the sun came up all the way.

When it was clear enough to see, I walked closer to the body. The sun was out strong so that even without the Hazmat suit, I didn't feel any flies.

When I got there, the body was gone. There was a trail where the dogs must have dragged her. In the trench that she made, there was something shiny.

I had a friend who lived in New York City during 9/11. He was one of the firemen who made it out. He saw so much destruction he could not talk about it. But we all knew the stories, teeth and bones found blocks away, being covered by debris that you knew was the decimated remains of people.

He only told me two things. One, that he didn't know why any of us were alive anyway.

"Come on, man," I remember I told him, "That's just the sadness talking. We're all sad like that."

"Why be sad?" he answered me, "Life's not even worth it."

The other thing that he told me was that, months after the attack, he would be walking down the street, and he'd see 11 pennies. Every day, he found 11 pennies in the street. Always in the configuration of one dime and one penny. Always 11 cents. This happened for two weeks, and then, on the last day, he found a nickel and six pennies all in a row on the sidewalk. He said his heart started to beat when he picked up the first nickel, went two steps and found a penny, and then another, until he got to 11 cents and the money stopped.

"What do you think it meant?" I asked him.

He shrugged. "I don't know. But that's the reason I get up every day, to see if it's going to happen again."

So the moment I saw the body gone and in her place something shiny, I went to see what it was. It was so strange because the muck around her body was so dull and covered with dusty debris. This shiny thing stood out, even though it must have been very small.

I stepped right over to where the depression was. There were no flies anymore. I bent to look down.

It was one shiny penny. Even though I didn't have on my gloves, I picked it up. It said 1995.

Suddenly, I felt every emotion I ever had—the sadness of my city gone, the confusion of fighting with my wife, and the pain of my friends back at the station. I knew they were now hurting because I hadn't returned. And I was overwhelmed by the number of people washed away from the Industrial Canal and others swept out of their homes to God knows where in the dark night. What about the families that we picked up in our boats, then dropped off dazed at all sorts of locations? There was the lack of food, water, electricity. It all hit me. And I sobbed. The water ran out of my eyes. The snot hung from my nose. My mouth wouldn't close. My uniform shirt was wet and useless. What is the use of fighting fires, when, every time, water is what kills us?

The penny in my hand slipped out to the ground.

I got on my hands and knees, and I asked God, "What kind of shit is this?"

And there was no answer from Him. Everything around me was nasty and quiet.

I waited. Nothing but silence. No dogs. No birds. Not even flies.

I got up and picked up a piece of newspaper to wipe my hands, and as I was throwing it away, I saw the headlines—genocide in Slovakia, mudslides in Mexico, active earthquakes and volcanoes.

Our tragedy was so ordinary that God didn't even bother to notice?

I thought of my only son.

He was unplanned. At first, I didn't want him. Then, he came out of my wife. He was slimy and bloody. He jittered like he was only half human but I suddenly wanted to pull him close to my chest so that my heart could beat for him. Breathe. Breathe. Breathe. Then, he cried, and I cried. But I didn't know whether I was happy or sad. Sad because I felt as if I had wasted my life until that moment. Happy because everything in the world would be different. I had discovered hope.

Now, I went back to pick through the muck that was generations of earth and trouble that God had forgot and the devil remade to find the penny again. I wanted to give it to my son. The date on the penny, 1995, was the year of his birth.

I found the coin and put it in my pocket, got my bat out of the car, and I started to walk toward the bridge. Around me was silence. The sky was so blue and so wide, I could hardly remember my name.

What Went Missing
and What Got Found

The crepe myrtles came back and so did the camellias. The magnolia and bay leaf that sat in water for many weeks died at the root. Tuber plants that everyone thought to be long gone revived. Four O'Clocks opened at sundown. People prayed that their bright yellow and pink flowers might bring back the hummingbirds.

I listened nightly for the manic beating of wings when I walked to my grandmother's house in the darkness. So far, it was still quiet.

In the day, I moved through the Seventh Ward neighborhood of single- and double-shotgun houses.

Most were damaged with shattered windows and a water line a quarter of the way up the outside walls. That's where the flood sat for weeks. It drove away the last generation who rode out the hurricanes in their homes and kept away most of the evacuees who normally would have returned by now, talking across their fences or laughing on a shared front porch with their parents.

From the Indian Market to the French Quarter and Congo Square, every important venue in this neighborhood carried the name of some ancestor. Claiborne, Prieur, Aubry, Johnson, and Roman were the names of the streets and also the surnames of their descendants. Their children had played on the sidewalks just before the storm. Now, children are the least apparent survivors. Block after block have only houses of men and the elderly.

I have returned to New Orleans from Washington, D. C. where I work for the Government Accountability Office. I have a well-paid contract to count the living and assess their needs since Katrina. But when I knock on each door and someone answers, his list is so long that it is just an exercise in naming.

Everything is gone—from refrigerators to tweezers, from tape to socks. I know, some people never had certain items such as electric clocks, tooth floss, or a safe, but I put these items down on the list for them.

They just may get some consolation prize for lasting it out.

For now, I offer them conversation. The woman at the airport counter talked to me about the lack of traffic when I picked up my baggage quickly from the empty carousel. At the rental car agency, the clerk told me about the way he is cooking meals for his father now that his mother died in the deluge. When I paid for gas to come into the city, the attendant told me about the water in his garage. I went straight to the downtown hotel to check in, where the clerk advised me that the time for happy hour was 4 p.m. It was 3:30 and people were already lined up.

"I'm not with the disaster tourists," I said.

"That don't mean nothing. Nobody will know," she said.

I got my key, then left.

When I left Washington, my lover, told me he could never live in a city like this.

"There aren't even any four-star restaurants," he said, only half-joking.

I went out last night and ordered Trout Almondine at a café with the benefit of electricity. The tables had an odd assortment of cloths and chairs. Customers were scattered in clumps like hair on a balding man's head. The streetcar clanged and screeched outside. The sound came uneasily through the open window.

The waitress approached me to say that she had only tap water, which she didn't trust enough to give me, and she had run out of bread. But the fish, she said, was freshly caught from the small streams upstate where they seemed to proliferate.

They were delicious. I wanted to tell my lover that I had a four-star dining experience. But I couldn't with only coffee and fish. Two stars fell automatically.

My car is a rental, and it smells like a plastic container. I am sweating from the heat outside. But I don't want to turn on the air conditioner and close the windows. I am afraid to preserve the toxins.

I asked my lover to accompany me to New Orleans.

"It's only temporary," I said.

"Don't I know it," he answered. "You'll see, you won't be able to last."

He cited the crime statistics, the lack of literacy, the alcoholism, and the inferior housing even prior to the storm.

"It's a money pit," he told me, "It breeds waste."

I was born in New Orleans. But I moved to Washington, D.C. more than two decades ago.

He was right, though. The only changes made in New Orleans seem to be because of Katrina. Before it, the houses were still unpainted, the screen doors torn, and the children barefoot. The same family names were listed on the sheet I received with assessments of narrow properties—thin houses with shoulder-width alleyways. The homes still held the latest generation of the city's first settlers—bureaucrats and businessmen or the people they owned. In this neighborhood they were both. The Seventh Ward was the crossroad of slaves and slave owners.

No other location in the city held that mix more apparently. It showed when the local school children visited the museums and saw their ancestors on the wall—with white faces. It came through the tales of grandmothers who told the younger generations about relatives they could not discuss in public. My own grandmother made me promise not to tell anyone that her mother wasn't married. I found out later that she was not married because the law did not allow miscegenation.

And now when I come back for the accounting, many secrets have died along with the earlier generations. No one knows the names of the people in grey photographs on crumbling sideboards or locked in chifferobes. Or that a chifferobe is the old name for an armoire.

After spending one night in the hotel, I decide to move into my grandmother's abandoned house. It is above the water line, and my cousins who lived there are now in Houston. They left oil in the kerosene lamp.

The next morning, I begin working. The first house I come to has an old lady and a dog. I wait and sweat on her porch. She tells me to come inside where it's shady.

"That sun ain't no good to nobody," she says.

"Yes, M'am." I take a seat on her one good chair. She brings a stool for herself and the dog sits on the floor beside her.

I know who she is, not really personally. But she has a familiar face. Perhaps she is the mother of one of my schoolmates.

"Done went to California," she says about her now-adult child. "Told me to come. I said, 'Not yet.'" She laughs, "I'll go when I'm dead."

I laugh with her because we both know that might not take too long. Humor is her only luxury.

I wonder about how the daughter reconciled leaving her mother alone in this climate.

The old woman answers for me, "I'm 93 now, and I rather die here than live in a foreign place."

The walls have clean white rectangles on them in a line at eye-level. Pictures are missing that had hung for years on the wall. All of the furniture appears to be in the front room. An oscillating fan, attached to a generator, keeps a breeze across our knees and lifts her skirt about every 20 seconds.

The window curtains are pulled back to bring in more air. The house alongside is visible. It is gutted, and rubble covers the yard. The old lady sits beside the window with her hands on her lap like Whistler's mother with a foreign war as the backdrop.

"The church children camed and help," she says when she sees me looking at the pile of trash just outside.

The volunteers from the North are everywhere.

They are pink-faced teenagers with white fiberglass masks. They wear rubber gloves, boots, and shorts. They tear through the rubble like rats.

"God bless them," the old woman says. "Good white people, still, in this day and age," she adds.

She was a soldier in the era of Civil Rights. She was one of the nameless then and now. We both know that she swallowed her pride and bit her tongue many times, and she stood on the slow bus going uptown so she could earn enough to raise that "girl" who lives now in California. Strange that integration brought opportunity and opportunity separated them.

I was a child here when these old people voted for their first black candidates in the 1970s. They continued voting for them until after the storm. Then they realized that the black politicians cared no more about them than the white ones.

Many old people drowned waiting for directions. Others died after the storm from disappointment.

I use a map that identifies the houses by measurements—the dimensions in feet and inches, lot sizes, and city squares. But I need very little guidance. I know these buildings from their foundations dug into the soft, dark mud to their raised plank floors to their high-pointed roofs that quickly wash away the rain. A shotgun house has two identical sides. The rooms go straight back, one behind the other. First a living room, then a bedroom or dining room, depending on the number of children, then bathroom, bedroom, and kitchen.

How many times did I bolt with my classmates after school through their family houses, only to be slowed and shushed at the door so that I would not wake a sleeping father in the second room lying crossways on the bed, exhausted from his night job? Or I sat knees together on the plastic-covered sofa in the first room while being served ice tea and a piece of cake, waiting to go to a dance with a double date friend. Her parents were so excited, and she would arrive like a wedding cake, layers of ruffles and sequins threaded in the center with tiny pearl beads. It would all come undone later in the backseat of a hot car. The beads rubbed off the seat of the dress would be re-sewn in the dark with a flashlight.

Sometimes in the back of a shotgun house, I would sit at someone's Formica table and eat hot fried chicken on thick paper plates. With a pitcher of lemonade in front of me and the back door open to create a breeze, I would laugh as loud as the others over the window fan.

The shotgun house, circa 1940, according to the map, doesn't begin to explain. Many of them are now empty, and just a few gutted. Most are simply vacant. The residents were big families, many with ties only occasionally documented in City Hall. They were bound by the heart which is now in pieces, so they scattered to the winds.

"Mother," I tell the old lady, "Let me get you some water from my car."

She looks hesitant, wondering whether I have taken this from the tap. Although she knows that the offer is well intended, the germs could kill her.

I add, "It's in the little bottles."

She nods yes, very quickly, as if I am offering her a diamond ring.

The oaks on nearby Esplanade keep the avenue cool as I walk to my next destination. I had a great interest in nature before I began working so far away. The golden rain tree in my grandfather's back yard dropped sheer little pods with tiny, brown seeds inside like messages in a bottle.

I climbed the cherry tree in my own backyard until I was 13 years old. Other girls my age were thinking of dating. But I was content in the early evening to sit in the high branches and look at the neighborhood.

On the corner was the Pastor's house. His daughter opened the long windows to her porch when she did her evening practice. First, I heard the piano and then her strong voice running the chords. First, third, fifth, eighth, fifth, third, first. In the spring, during the Creole Fiesta, she and her father performed a duet on the porch before the champagne toast. I stood among the neighbors thinking this is what people mean when they say elegance.

Farther down the block was the school where my mother worked. I could hear them too on a quiet day. The noon bell rang and, in the afternoon, children sang their times tables. At three o'clock, the bell rang again, and their voices roared tumbling out of the metal double doors. Then quickly all of the noise dissipated.

I marked time by these neighborhood comings and goings. Eight a.m., children went to school. Noon, their bell rang. Three p.m., they flooded the sidewalks for home. Four p.m., the church bells rang for mass. Six p.m., the Pastor's daughter practiced. Then the block was silent again. I spent years listening to the lives of others.

Then, I moved away quickly before anyone discovered that I had begun to count time in months. My tranquility disappeared after one boy and one night. I had started a life of my own.

Blossoming trees and dead branches now encircle the Seventh Ward. It is an area where everyone knows my name. My father's father and my father lived in these houses. My mother grew up here too. They met in the eighth grade.

The first roads into this neighborhood were already cleared by the 1800s. A large street near my house is called Bayou Road as if its discoverers knew they would never part with the water.

Now, a year after the flood, the path that the water took through the houses still remains. I can follow the mud ruts from the front door through to the backyard. In some houses, the owners came back to empty the furniture and scrape down to whatever remained of the floors and the walls.

The houses that no one has touched aren't approachable without a mask for sanitation and sanity. The water mashed all the contents. The rubble is rotten and moldy. It's like the inside of a rancid refrigerator whose perishables could be a friend.

Sometimes, the water washed through the front rooms of houses, picked up families and tossed them into the street. Husband and wife were separated, sometimes floating individually to death. Others made it out alive but could never return. They went to live alone in dry apartments. They survived but wonder why.

I can go street after street, and there are no lights in the homes. It doesn't matter whether they are brick or frame, they stand or were flattened on the impulse of the wind. I used to think God caused all this destruction. Then I began to believe in science. Barometric pressure and water temperature cause the swirling clouds that suck the heart out of the Gulf and deposit the mass on the ground. The one thing I don't understand is if science is so precise, why is destruction so random?

In Washington, I took to the hospital bed when my teenaged pregnancy didn't last. The nurses had no interest. I could hear their conversations in the middle of the night over the ward. They talked about pay raises and pensions, health insurance and vacation days.

I thought that I called out to one of them. But I could never tell who came to my bed. Their faces floated, disconnected from their bodies, and they addressed me as if my brain was addled.

"My baby," I remember thinking, "will never be." I wanted to ask for what remained of her after she washed away. But the question never formed into words.

In New Orleans, the week after the flood, everything was covered with mud. When it dried, it cracked into little patterns with scales that rose up on the hottest days, and finally crumbled back to dust.

Now, I return to my grandmother's house at night. So far, it is the only place I can rest.

The house creaks from different corners of every room like wood talking to wood. They quip briefly and then there are long silences. The wood's conversations are not unlike those of my grandparents. My grandfather would arrive in the evening and grunt for dinner. My grandmother answered him by lowering his heavy plate to the oak table with finality.

There was security in knowing that every day would be the same. I was able to fit into the spaces of quiet between them.

I stayed in Washington. Too ashamed to come home, I finished school there. I got a job. My failure stuck to my bones. I stayed gone.

I am my lover's assistant. I go to his dark office, paneled in imported wood. I have a desk at the door. His agenda is predictable and unrelenting. First to the coffee shop, then to the morning meeting, then to the phone calls, video-conferences, lunches, meetings, and cocktail parties or dinners. Afterwards, I stumble home with him, up the marble steps of his white townhouse.

He puts his neat suit on a chair, and I put it away into a closet of similarly pressed clothes. He has a tie for every day of the month. I watch him arrange and undo the knots around his slim neck. Sometimes his ties send messages to his constituents—vote yes or vote no or wait until I tell you what to do. I am good at interpreting his thoughts.

The next day in New Orleans, I visit a man with a bottle of port wine in the kitchen. He asks me to drink with him before we begin to talk.

"What are you missing?" I ask him formally because obviously everything is gone.

"I don't miss anything," he tells me. The things that he had, he says, he never needed. The things that people bring him are gifts, also unnecessary.

"I make everything I want," he adds and shows me an old box constructed from rescued wood. He says that inside of it are his food, his clothes, and his medicine. He waves his hand around the room, clean now down to the scraped plaster walls. A bed sits against one of them. There is a rocking chair and a table. There is a radio. The newspaper and a Bible sit on the floor next to a cup of water.

He has two mugs, and he fills both of them half way with the port. It is a hot day, and I begin sweating. We are the only people on the block, but I am not afraid to be alone with him. I know him. He is a liar.

"Do you have family?" I ask. "Children?"

"I had children once. But I don't know where they're at," he says to me. "They went off with their mother to Chicago, and they don't call. Sometimes they visit, but I never know when."

He tips his cup to mine, and I look at him carefully before downing the heavy drink.

The wine, at first, feels refreshing, then, it burns in the pit of my stomach.

"My children," he continues, "I guess they were mine. They lived in my house. I fed them. I taught them as much as I could. But, for some reason, they didn't listen."

"I'm sure they listened some."

"They listened too much, if you ask me." I see the port was working already. "They listened when I told their mother to go her own way. They went with her. You can't live with some women," he says. "No offense," he adds.

"I don't take any," I say. I lie now along with him.

By the time I leave his house, he has finished the bottle. One drink and my head is swimming. I am wobbling as I walk to my grandmother's home.

The sidewalks are cracked. And there are huge holes in the street where the tar has given away. I measure the pace of my gait by the number of times I hear cars try to zip past me then bang and bump into the holes.

First the front end hits. Then, the back end. In between, the driver becomes aware of his mistake.

Either because of driver error or terrible fate, car accidents are common around New Orleans now, even in its empty state. Cars run into each other in the dark at stop lights that are no longer there. Cars regularly pick up debris, pieces of glass, and nails that pierce their tires, ending their drivers' progress.

Tonight, after I sober a little, I get in the car and go to the hotel where I use the computer to send a report back to the office. In the lobby, there is too much mirth. Contractors, bankers, and other white collar specialists are glad to be completing their tasks, and going back to their homes in the North and Midwest. Glad to have picked up a contract. Glad to have met similar strangers.

They don't talk about what was lost, but what can be done. They have reasonable plans with futuristic rationales. They know so little.

They talk about building condos on the lakefront, yet they have never walked into the water. They have never tasted its salty waves or stepped on its muddy shell bottom. If they ever swam in it, they would know its warmth and buoyancy. They would know the kinds of fish in the lake that come up to the shore and do not swim away. Drum, mullet, and catfish make this lakeshore unlike Orlando, Virginia Beach, or Cape Town, South Africa. The men at the hotel talk of waterfront vistas that can be purchased, shored up, and sold.

Commerce is not how we think.

In high school, we sat like birds on a wall watching the tide. It went out in the evening, taking the sun. More people flocked to the seawall as the evening wore on, listening to the sounds of the waves and buzzing mosquitos. It gave way to the sounds of laughter, and then whispering later.

Couples sat in their cars talking about the dreams that the lake conjured. Houses and families imagined by the outlines of dark clouds catching the moonlight. Ambitions were summoned by stars. Friends and lovers talked quietly about the future, knowing there would be New Orleans to return to, no matter who they would become. For some who would never leave, there was always only New Orleans.

Picnics on the lake, barbeques, touch football games. Parties that went back to the house, where the same dances were performed by members of every generation. Teenagers doing the swings and clutches of the Lindy Hop. Uncles shrugging their shoulders and sliding along the floor to mimic the latest style. Mothers swaying off to the kitchen to bring out more food and more.

The hotel bar announces its last call to the lobby. It is an announcement I never heard before in New Orleans. Anyone could sit at a bar until the sun rose. The big question then was whether the bar cooked breakfast or whether it was served around the corner.

A man asks me to join him for a drink and wants my telephone number.

I smile and walk in the opposite direction.

He calls after me like a ship with a new bell, unseasoned and with no resonance.

I get into my car and drive through the dark streets. There are no streetlights. The stop signs are all twisted. Some are leaning off to the side. Some are upside down. None are reliable.

Everything has stopped already. There should be signs that say, "Go," "Go carefully," and "Go with God."

At the most popular intersections, I am the only person. In Washington, I might be afraid that there is someone hiding in the shadows. But in New Orleans, after the hurricane, I know, for sure, I am alone.

My lover will never miss me. He needs someone carefree. That's the way I once appeared. I am aging now by the moment.

How much time will it take to repair New Orleans' damage? For an acorn to replace a fallen oak tree? How many generations before a flood turns from memory to myth to be rediscovered as history? Everyone here can tell me a story. They call it reality.

Why did my child come into being, then disappear? If I could have stopped thinking perhaps the answer would have come to me.

If I ever conceive a child again, I will bring it before God. I will hold Him to my prayers. I will talk like the people of the Old Testament, "God, you promised . . ." He told me that He would take care of me, and He didn't. He knows he didn't.

I stop at a place I knew long ago. My uncles and cousins went there after a night of drinking. It was a place for men to become quiet. They did not have lovers. They had wives who stayed at home and waited for them to purge their demons before laying eyes on their children.

There are empty houses on either side of the bar when I arrive. There are no lights in the street. There are no people outside. I get out of my car. I look at the landscape I used to know. It is barren. The smell of rot is all around. I can just barely smell the salty air from the nearby lake.

Still, as I approach the building, I see there are cars parked in the back. They sit on the broken sidewalk and are jammed near the rubble.

I open the door to the bar which is even more humid than the temperature outside. All of the faces inside turn to look at me. They have the hopeful expressions I remember. There are women I know, heavier, rounder, and happier than I recall. Something in this destruction has given them purpose. Maybe it's the chance to start over. Maybe it's just that they are alive.

I go inside and the band is about to play. Someone offers me a chair and a hug. It is a woman I barely recognize. "We are happy to see you home," she says to me.

This is home to all of them whether the flood comes or the houses blow away. They are here. They will rebuild it one cup, one fork, one plate at a time. They are doubtless.

I smell a whiff of blood, and I think that it's mine. It wafts like a spirit then disappears.

A man reaches for my hand to dance.

"I can see that we have a lot in common," he says. He points to his dark brows and full lips, "You are just like me."

I remember this kind of opening line from when I was a teenager. A young man approached my girlfriend with the line, "We'd make beautiful children."

He looked like he could have been her brother. Dark eyes, narrow faces. Both of them had smooth, youthful skin and elderly, round shoulders. They did look like each other. She agreed to go out, and later she married him.

I thought she was being easy. Now, I wonder. What did she know about life? And what have I learned?

The music begins to play. The people get up from their seats. They are still in their work clothes. Some men are splattered with paint. Others have muddy shoes.

The contrast between them and my lover is striking. I am thrown momentarily off balance as if the universe has reversed its rotation.

I shakily take the hand of the man from my neighborhood. He pulls me close. He leans toward my face and whispers a simple question in my ear. What he asks goes to my core.

"Are you happy?" he asks.

At first, I wonder if this is a real question. Then, does it matter? Then, what if the words that I use right now make it true? So I answer with faith.

"Now, I am."

Then, the music plays, and I remove myself from his arms. I spin out to the dance floor and snap my fingers. I begin again.

What Went Missing

Acknowledgements

Many thanks to Xavier Review Press, Saint Peter's University and the Writers Room for support with this book. Also, thanks to the Kittredge Fund, the LEH and the NEH for research assistance. I am grateful for the good people around me including my WNBA and PEN American Center friends, Marie Brown, Executive Editor Nicole Greene and Editors Ralph Adamo, Katheryn Laborde, Tom Bonner, and Robert Skinner at the Xavier Review, and, for early encouragement, James Olney at the Southern Review and writers Al Young and Terry McMillan. I also wish to thank friends and readers of my early drafts Diane Simmons, Kaitlyn and Alexi Gaddis, Elizabeth Moore Rhodes, Rhona Whitty, Marlene Veloso, Lisa Bergson, Rebecca Tabb, Esq., Lauren Fleitas, Kavery Kaul, and Pamela Tabb. Much love and appreciation to James, Celeste and Sophia for always listening and helping.

About the Author

Fatima Shaik writes fiction and non-fiction for adults and children. Her work has appeared in *The Southern Review*, *Callaloo*, *Essence*, *Tribes*, the *Review of Contemporary Fiction* and *The New York Times*. She is included in several anthologies including *Streetlights: Illuminating Tales of the Urban Black Experience* (Penguin), *Breaking Ice: An Anthology of Contemporary African American Fiction* (Penguin-Viking), and *N.O. Lit: 200 Years of New Orleans Literature* (Lavender Ink). She is the recipient of awards from the National Endowment for the Humanities, Louisiana Endowment for the Humanities and the Kittredge Fund.

She is an assistant professor at Saint Peter's University and a native of New Orleans.

Also by Fatima Shaik

The Mayor of New Orleans: Just Talking Jazz

The Jazz of Our Street

On Mardi Gras Day

Melitte

CPSIA information can be obtained
at www.ICGtesting.com
Printed in the USA
LVOW04s0340041215
465307LV00019B/172/P